SO-CTB-277

Darkness at the Door

*Other Five Star Titles
by Catherine Dain:*

Angel in the Dark
Death of the Party

Darkness at the Door

A New Age Mystery

Catherine Dain

Five Star • Waterville, Maine

Five Star First Edition Mystery Series.

Published in 2001 in conjunction with Tekno Books and Ed Gorman.

Set in 11 pt. Plantin.

Printed in the United States on permanent paper.

Library of Congress Cataloging-in-Publication Data

Dain, Catherine.
　　Darkness at the door : a New Age mystery / Catherine Dain.
　　　　p. cm. — (Five Star first edition mystery)
　　ISBN 0-7862-3553-5 (hc : alk. paper)
　　1. Psychics — Fiction.　I. Title.　II. Series.
　　PS3554.A32 D37 2001
　　813'.54—dc21
　　　　　　　　　　　　　　　　　　　　2001050172

Darkness at the Door

Prologue

She stood barefoot on the white sand, dressed in a loose white tunic, looking out at the deep blue water that stretched unruffled to the horizon, where it met a pale blue sky. A few wispy clouds drew her eyes up and over to the west.

The dragon ship was coming, gliding to shore, though its sails were hanging limply and no hands were at the oars.

She stepped forward into the cool water. Her bare feet sank into the sand, and the waves swirled gently around her ankles.

The green and golden dragon's head nodded in greeting, its painted eyes glistening.

The vessel stopped a few feet in front of her. She waded close enough to steady herself against the neck of the carved dragon and climb in. The dragon ship glided back out to sea and carried her into the mist.

She was barely aware of the changes in her body, but by the time the dragon ship left the mist and deposited her on another shore, she had become a young man, still dressed in the same white tunic, still barefoot.

A few tentative steps forward swirled the landscape and brought him suddenly into an amphitheater.

His white tunic was now covered by a long purple robe, and his feet had stepped into awkward platform sandals, built to lift him off the ground. A mask covered his face.

He was speaking, and other actors answered, even though his words didn't reach his own ears.

He made his exit and stood, waiting for his cue to reenter.

But another figure in mask and robe was next to him. A hand slipped under his mask to stop his voice, and a knife slipped between his ribs to stop his heart. He struggled to see the face behind the mask. Not even the eyes were clear to him.

He could feel the blood pumping out, feel himself becoming lighter, floating back to the dragon ship, back into the mist, changing back into a woman . . .

The ship left her where it had found her, standing on the white beach.

Who . . .

Chapter One

Hello!

The word popped into Mariana's head as she stepped onto the grass.

Hello, Dorothy, she sent back. *I'll be there in a minute.*

Hello, Mary. Hello, Hiram, Walter, Juan. She formed the names in her mind as she passed the flat bronze plaques, her back bent slightly as she climbed the slope toward Dorothy's grave. They didn't acknowledge her presence, and Mariana had never searched for their energy forms, even though she was fairly certain that Dorothy wasn't the only spirit who had chosen to stay with her bones.

She felt a slight rumbling coming from the direction of the General's grave. She ignored it, as she always did. Something about the General's rumblings kept her from talking to him —she might get trapped into listening to old war stories.

Mariana had discovered Cemetery Park—and Dorothy —not long after she moved to Ventura. She had needed to walk, needed a reason to leave her apartment besides going to work at Enchantment, needed a destination. The square block of bright green grass studded with an incongruous mix of juniper, live oak, cypress, and palm trees was just over a mile from where she lived.

The first time she walked up the stone steps from Main Street, she hadn't realized that the park was an old cemetery.

It appeared to be nothing more than a well tended, but seldom used, patch of public greenery. The random bronze plaques were a surprise.

Dorothy was buried next to Alice and Thomas, her parents. Mariana had found the three graves under a large spreading evergreen when she was looking for a shady place to sit for a moment before starting back. From the gravesite she could look across housetops to the Pacific Ocean and the Channel Islands. The afternoon breeze had cleared the sky of clouds, so water and air were almost the same bright blue. A lone white sail spoke of a truant sailor, unable to resist the beauty of a Friday morning in early October.

Mariana had settled cross-legged onto the grass and thought, hello, Dorothy. She hadn't really expected Dorothy to answer. But Dorothy welcomed her so warmly that Mariana had come to visit frequently since.

Dorothy shared a few images with her during the intervening months, enough to explain that she was happy, that she didn't want to move on, didn't want to come back to a new life. Once Mariana made the mistake of sitting on the grave, and Dorothy had taken the opportunity to share the experience of her death in childbirth, at age twenty. Mariana was careful to sit next to the grave from then on.

Hello!

Hello, Dorothy.

Dorothy wasn't much of a conversationalist—Mariana suspected that she hadn't been very bright when she was alive, and death hadn't increased her wisdom—but she liked having Mariana visit, as long as Mariana was quiet. Speaking out loud changed the vibration, and Dorothy disappeared.

The year is winding down, Mariana thought. Halloween this month, then Thanksgiving, then Christmas. She would have to decide what to do for the holidays.

Dorothy offered a picture of how happy she had been sharing holidays with her parents.

I know, Mariana thought, I know you were happy. But not everyone enjoys spending time with her parents.

Dorothy didn't respond.

Mariana shut her eyes. She would have offered a full-throated *Om* to the heavens, but Dorothy didn't like the way chanting altered the energy in the park. Didn't want to call attention to herself, Mariana thought. Someone might want her to evolve.

A soccer ball hit Dorothy's marker and bounced past Mariana's face.

"Sorry!"

A prepubescent girl in white T-shirt and shorts dashed to retrieve it.

"Not a problem."

But it was. The park was starting to fill with eleven-year-old soccer players. The school, about two blocks away, had no grassy field for them to practice on, so the gym classes came out to play on sunny days.

Mariana didn't like watching them running around on the graves, but Dorothy didn't seem to mind.

I'm leaving, Mariana thought. *I'll come again soon. Good-bye.*

Mariana stood, pausing to take a last look at the water. Then she headed on up the hill to Poli, turning right toward the nearby Presbyterian Church, a tawny stucco building with echoes of missionary architecture. She thought every once in a while about stopping, asking if anyone at the church could tell her about Dorothy, or what had happened to Dorothy's baby, but she hadn't done it. Ventura was full of ghosts, and most of the human residents seemed pretty matter-of-fact about sharing the city with them.

Still, the church might not appreciate the questions. And if she did find Dorothy's son—or grandson—what would she say? It wasn't as if Dorothy had a message for anyone. Or as if she even really remembered the baby. She had died before bonding with him. And it had been so long ago. Just after the turn of the last century. Before the First World War.

Mariana walked on, passing stucco bungalows with red tile roofs and climbing purple bougainvillea, and compact frame houses with lush rose bushes, some bright pink, some flame-tipped yellow, that kept their blooms long into what passed for autumn in the rest of the northern hemisphere. She envied the people who lived in the houses for what she imagined was a stable life, with stable relationships, envied their yards and their views of the sparkling waves.

At least today whoever lived there had views. Many days the marine layer was so heavy that the water turned gray and the islands disappeared in fog.

But that meant Ventura was gloriously cool. On days when she didn't feel like walking to the cemetery, Mariana drove to the beach. Even in September, usually the hottest month in Southern California, there had only been a few days when the sun was so hot that the beach was out of the question.

Mariana turned down Lincoln to cross Main at the stoplight. Ventura was a quiet town with a low crime rate, but there was still an occasional hit-and-run accident, and Main was the closest thing to a busy street in midtown.

She lost track of the ocean once she passed Main. Houses and palm trees—and the railroad line and the freeway—all came between.

Her brother, Brian. Dead. His face twisted in pain. Blood from the hole in his chest had soaked into his shirt and his

12

jeans, until they were no longer white or blue but deep purplish red.

Her heart began pounding, and she opened her mouth to scream. But the flesh melted from the bones, and then the corpse vanished, before she released the sound.

"Oh, God." The scream had dwindled to a whimper.

She stared at the sidewalk and worked to control her breath, forcing air in, pushing it out, rhythmically, to still her heart. Her hands moved to her chest, almost without her willing it, to encourage a calming energy.

"Hawk? Will you tell me something about him now?"

The spirit bird, the messenger guide who brought her information, was silent.

When Mariana was certain she could control her legs, she walked the last block and a half to her apartment. She had found a quiet space in an alley, over a garage, taking the first place she looked at from an ad in the local paper, knowing that a housing angel was guiding her. She fumbled for the keys as she climbed the stairs.

Ella was just inside the door, yelling at the top of her lungs, the you-abandoned-me-and-left-me-to-starve yell. Mariana was still shaking from her vision, and she wanted to curl up in bed. Instead, she picked up the howling Siamese and carried her through the hall and into the kitchen.

"I fed you before I left," she said. The bowl was empty, though. Feeding Ella required finding the line between giving her so little that she wanted more and giving her so much that it went to waste. Ella wouldn't eat anything that had been sitting more than an hour—she saw it as the cat equivalent of road kill, and she didn't eat carrion. Mariana put the slender cat on the kitchen counter and spooned a little more canned turkey-and-whatever into a bowl.

Miles, a brown-and-white domestic long hair with the robust body of a Maine coon cat, rubbed against her leg to let her know that his dish was empty, too. Miles would gladly finish anything that Ella left, but he was already fat enough that sometimes he took a second try to reach the counter.

"You had enough," Mariana said, trying to steady her voice. "Ella is too thin, but you're too fat. And I have to get ready to go to work."

The cat's expression was so pained that she relented.

"Only one more bite," she warned.

The bite, really a spoonful, was gone in an instant.

She did have to get ready to go to work. But she couldn't get rid of the image of Brian on the sidewalk.

Keeping an eye on Miles to discourage him from even thinking about jumping up on the counter to eat whatever Ella might leave behind, Mariana picked up the kitchen phone and punched the familiar number.

"Welcome to Enchantment," Deirdre's voice said.

"I'm not sure I can work today," Mariana said. "I had a vision—"

"Tell me about it when you get here," Deirdre said, cutting her off. "You're a professional now, Mariana, and you have readings scheduled. I don't want to call people and cancel appointments because a psychic can't handle her own visions. Take a mental shower and clean your chakras. And I'll see you in an hour."

The phone clicked in Mariana's ear. She still wanted to curl up in bed, but Deirdre had annoyed her enough that she decided to try another way of handling the vision. She punched another number into the phone.

"Have you heard from Brian?" she asked, when her mother answered.

Mariana held her breath as she waited for the response.

"Brian? Oh, God, Mariana. I haven't heard from Brian for

more than two years." Linda's voice fluttered with age and pain. "If I had heard from him, I would surely have let you know. Why are you asking? Did you pick something up?"

"I thought I saw him," Mariana hedged, "but then he faded."

"I don't understand why you can't come up with something better than that. You say you're a psychic, and he's your twin brother. What good does it do you to be a psychic if you can't find your own brother?" She paused only long enough for emphasis. "Was he in trouble?"

"Sort of, yes. Nothing clear." Mariana decided not to tell Linda about the bloody corpse. "And I've told you before, it's hard for a psychic to pick up anything when she has a stake in the outcome. I care too much."

"I know you care, and I don't understand why that makes it harder, not easier. And I hope you're wrong." Linda trilled the word, giving it added weight. "I hope he's all right, wherever he is."

"I do, too. Really."

Linda's voice cracked again. "But if he's all right, I don't understand why he doesn't get in touch. He was so talented, so intelligent, so handsome, he could have done anything, been anything he wanted." The flutter in her voice turned into a moan.

"I don't know why he doesn't get in touch. I only asked if you'd heard from him." Mariana had trouble listening when her mother began keening over Brian. "I can't stay on the phone—I have to go to work."

"All right." Linda shut down. "No. No, I haven't heard from him, not since the postcard from Wyoming, however long ago that was. Are you really making any money? I do wish you'd get a job."

"Some. Getting better. And it is a job. It just isn't what

you consider a job."

"You're right, it isn't."

"How's Todd?"

"Your father is fine. I'm sure he'd like to see you. Are you coming down for Thanksgiving? I need to know before I get the turkey. If it's just the two of us, I'll only get a breast." Linda paused, then added, "Your father does love you, you know that."

"I know that." Mariana wanted to point out that it wasn't even Halloween yet, plenty of time to plan for Thanksgiving, but she didn't want to get into an argument. "Tell him I'm planning to come."

It was emotional blackmail. Especially when Thanksgiving was still several weeks away. The mark of how desperately awful the family get-togethers were, was how much Linda insisted on them and how much Mariana tried to avoid them. And how much both thought about them. The blackmail was effective nevertheless.

"But you still don't need to get more than a breast," she added. "I'll be happy with salad and side dishes."

"I don't know why you have to be a vegetarian for Thanksgiving."

"I'm a vegetarian every day. Although I don't feel too sorry for turkeys. If I were going to eat meat, it would be turkey. They've been bred to be so dumb that they're practically vegetables." When her mother didn't comment, Mariana said, "I'll call you before, and I'll see you then."

Mariana hung up the phone, wondering whether she should have told Linda the substance of the vision after all. But it wasn't easy for her to talk with her mother about her psychic abilities, about her attempts to understand and control them. They didn't talk very often, and Mariana tried to avoid confrontation when they did, but too often the conversations turned into harangues about how Mariana was or was not making a living.

Not while Tim was alive, of course. Mariana had been a writer, which Linda had accepted as long as Mariana worked for a magazine, had a steady job. And Linda had grudgingly accepted Mariana's decision to freelance because, in Linda's eyes, Tim's career as a studio musician was the important one.

After Tim's death, Mariana had tried teaching, which would have been fine with Linda, but Mariana hadn't felt she was very good at it. Trying to sell her services as a freelance writer hadn't really worked either, because she found it hard to keep selling herself. Worse, she had lost her enthusiasm for writing. She kept her journal still, a lifetime habit, but it had been more than a year since she had written anything else.

Linda hadn't liked it when Mariana first told her that she was giving psychic readings. She even seemed pleased, vindicated, when Mariana hit a bad spell and couldn't hear her guides.

Mariana, however, had been devastated. She was on the verge of making a living as a psychic, but the voices suddenly became silent, and she stopped accepting appointments.

Then Deirdre called. Deirdre, a psychic channel who had also lost her husband to violence, was buying a metaphysical store in Ventura called Enchantment.

"I can't do everything myself, run the store, teach classes, give readings," Deirdre said. "Why don't you move out here and help me?"

"Because I've gone dry," Mariana answered. "I can't help."

"Oh, nonsense. Too much happened to you, that's all. Your psychic gifts snapped into place too suddenly. Of course you panicked—delayed shock. But you'll love

Ventura, you'll see. I'll help you with a tool to make readings easier—you could pick up tarot in no time—and you really need to appoint one of your guides as a gatekeeper, so that you don't get too many voices talking at once, which means that you don't hear any of them clearly." Deirdre kept talking until she convinced Mariana to come for a visit.

And Deirdre was right. Mariana fell in love with the city. Deirdre was also right about her talents. In the small store, amid the jewelry and the crystals and the incense and the candles, Mariana discovered she could read again. Now, though, her spirit guide was a hawk. Her tool was a deck of tarot cards. And she received images more than words.

The move to Ventura had helped everything. Slowly, surely, the information was starting to flow, and the clients were coming.

Ella butted her head against Mariana's side, letting her know she had finished eating and wanted more attention. Mariana hugged the cat for a moment before setting her down on the kitchen floor. Ella had only left a little in the dish, so Mariana gave it to the patient—if fat—Miles, who had quickly finished his own. He purred as he snapped it up, thanking her for her efforts on his behalf.

"You're welcome," she said.

She left the cats in the kitchen and walked back through the narrow hall to her bedroom. When she had moved—her second move in little more than a year—she had stripped down to necessities. The bedroom held her bed, a small chest, and her pink meditation chair. The bed was against the northwest corner of the room, under a *feng shui* crystal, with a nightstand and lamp next to it. The nightstand that should have gone on the other side of the bed sat next to her chair. She wasn't planning to have overnight company.

She had begun an affair after Tim died, even as her psychic talents were exploding, but it hadn't worked any better than anything else in her life at that time. In fact the affair, with Art Freeman, who had been one of her students, was part of what convinced her that she shouldn't be teaching. Then there was just too much happening, too many things changing, to invest in a new love. Or a new career, for that matter.

Mariana had kept her beloved museum posters, the Georgia O'Keeffe and the Matisse, but there was still a Spartan quality, not only to the bedroom, but to the whole apartment. The few visitors she'd had, none of whom knew her before the move, commented on how many books were on the living room shelves. Any visitor who did know her would have commented on how few. The Friends of the Library had gratefully accepted the boxes of books she no longer wanted.

Ella darted past her and waited by the pink chair, poised to leap if Mariana sat.

"Okay," Mariana said. She had been heading for the bed, but the cat was reinforcing Deirdre's suggestion. Take a mental shower, clean your chakras, and go to work. "I'll sit for a minute with you. But then I have to get to the store."

Mariana settled cross-legged into the wide chair, hands on her knees. The cat hopped up, circled twice, then curled up on Mariana's ankles.

"*Om.*" Mariana drew out the word, repeating it three times, softly, not with the full voice she really wanted to use. Her neighbors were too close, and sound carried easily.

She concentrated on her breath, in and out, allowed her body to relax. As thoughts came into her head, she let them go without comment. Even the thought carrying a hope that a guide would take pity, would offer information about Brian, she let that one go, too.

Silence. Silence, except for her own inner voice, the voice that is always there.

No guide, no angel would let her know where he was.

She probed for Brian's spirit and couldn't find it. That gave her some hope. Surely, if Brian were dead, he would find a way to talk to her.

The thought that he would find a way to talk if he were alive came and went.

Another thought came and went, that the reason she visited Dorothy so often was simply that when she said hello, Dorothy always answered. Dorothy didn't play games.

Mariana shifted her focus from her breath to the image of a garden with a waterfall. She visualized herself stepping into the waterfall, and then, still breathing quietly, visualized the water changing to the colors of the rainbow, and the colored water cleaning her chakras.

"I got a peaceful, easy feeling . . ."

That voice was outside her head, and loud, jerking her out of her meditation.

Ella leapt to the floor in annoyance.

One of Mariana's neighbors had a tendency to turn up the CD player when she cleaned house. The vacuum cleaner would start soon. Mariana couldn't fault her neighbor for cleanliness or for taste in music—everyone loves the Eagles, she thought—and she felt she couldn't complain when, after all, the only thing interrupted was a meditation that would have ended shortly anyway.

"Oh, shit," she muttered to herself.

Music had been part of her life during her marriage. Tim had something on all the time, usually classic jazz, but everything up to and including Pink Floyd and Cowboy Junkies. She had even learned to write while there was music in the background. Now she had become accustomed to silence.

Music was a reminder of her old life, and she only listened in the car. The car radio played easy listening music, the kind that helped her to stay calm, no matter what the driving conditions.

She stood up, stretched her legs, and wondered if she had anything, if Brian had ever given her anything that might explain his disappearance. Or her vision.

She wondered if Brian really were dead. And she realized that she had no faith in the clarity of the vision. Brian could be alive or dead, but her vision by itself meant nothing without confirmation. Six months earlier, she would have believed in the sight. Since then she had learned what an imperfect channel she was, and she simply didn't know what to believe, especially when her meditation came up empty.

The hall closet held the boxes that would have been stored in the garage if she had a garage to store them in. One of them might have something she could seize on, a sign, an omen, a clue, or just something that would help her tune to Brian's vibration.

The boxes weren't labeled. She had to pull out four-year-old income tax information, the Christmas decorations she kept in case she ever decided to observe the holiday again, and the few sentimental things she kept when her grandmother's house was sold, before she found the box of memories.

She didn't know what else to call it.

Photographs, letters, newspaper clippings. Stuff.

First, she needed photographs, the childhood envelope that was down near the bottom of the box.

Two brown-eyed, tow-headed toddlers playing in the sand. Laughing. Brian stuck his head in a pail, she hit the pail with a shovel, both of them thought it was funny. Mariana shut her eyes, remembering Brian's laugh, remembering the warmth of his small child body as they rolled together in the sand.

She had thought they would always be together. In those days she had no concept to match the word "alone."

She opened her eyes to a rare shot of her father, Todd, who usually held the camera, with Brian tugging on one hand, Mariana tugging on the other.

Then one of Linda chasing the twins out of the water, no one smiling.

Mariana had forgotten how distant and fearful Linda had been, even when she and Brian were children. But there it was.

All the pictures were of childhood, twins hugging and whispering and loving each other, never apart. She ached with longing for that closeness. There was no adolescence envelope, and she didn't bother to search for other pictures. Linda had suffered a bout of depression, and Todd had stopped taking pictures. That was when her parents had become Linda and Todd to her, not Mom and Dad. That was when she and Brian learned to fend for themselves.

Mariana was about to close that box to look for a high school yearbook in another—there had to be some trace of adolescent memories in the closet—when a postcard landed in her hand. A waterfall, lush foliage, and pink flowers. She turned it over.

Hi! How are you! I am on vacation in Maui, and I was thinking about you. I'll call you soon. Love, Brian.

Three years ago. She had only seen him once after he returned.

She shut her eyes, postcard in her hands.

The only vibrations on the postcard were from the box it had been lying in. Nothing of Brian.

She tossed it back.

When she last saw Brian, she and Tim were living in that funky Echo Park apartment. Tim was still alive. And she realized that the vision of the bleeding body on the sidewalk was one that she used to have of Tim. It was from the nightmare she had right after he was murdered. That calmed her more than the chakra cleansing.

She had come to terms with her husband's murder, or at least had found some serenity when she knew his spirit had risen, but now, for some reason, she had substituted her twin brother's body in his place, with a knife wound instead of a bullet wound.

Brian is probably alive, Mariana thought. Really he is.

The three of them—Mariana, Tim, and Brian—had gone out for dinner, and Brian talked about moving to Sedona. He was certain he would find the teacher he wanted in Sedona, the one who would help him find enlightenment in this lifetime. Somewhere in the box was a postcard from Sedona telling her that he was moving on, would give her an address when he had one.

She had tried to find him in Sedona after she began to have psychic experiences. No one she talked with there had ever heard of him.

But she didn't have time to look for the Sedona postcard. Anyway, Linda's Wyoming postcard came several months later. And there was no return address on it. And Mariana had to stop thinking about Brian.

She barely had time to clean herself up, change into a long flowered skirt and a ruffled pink blouse, and leave for the store. Deirdre would be waiting for her.

Mariana felt the hawk settle onto her shoulder as she locked the door to the apartment.

You'll tell me what the people who come for readings want to know, Mariana thought. Why won't you tell me what I want to know?

The spirit guide was silent.

Someone was calling. She couldn't see, but she could hear, and she knew the voice belonged to a child, a boy, with brown skin and shaggy black hair.

She reached out, trying to touch him, and their hands almost met.

Chapter Two

The first time Mariana walked into Enchantment, she realized that Deirdre was right in asking for help, and not simply because being the mother of two preadolescent children meant that Deirdre couldn't live in the back room. Deirdre had to leave at night, had to have a home to go to.

This was a larger operation than the store in Chatsworth had been, the one where Mariana and Deirdre had met. The Aquarian Moon had consisted of two rooms, a larger one for merchandise and a smaller one for classes and readings, plus a tiny two-room living space for the proprietor.

But Deirdre bought a going concern, kept the name Enchantment, and put her own stamp on it. One room held the usual collection found at metaphysical stores—books, crystals, incense, jewelry, tarot cards, and so on—although Deirdre's taste in jewelry resulted in a better selection than most. Beyond that were five more rooms. One was a combination storage room and office, one was reserved for psychic readings. Two were rented out as offices for a hypnotherapist and a Reiki master healer who was also an herbalist. The fifth was a classroom.

Deirdre had managed to get something scheduled in the classroom almost every night of the week. Thursday nights were taken by the hypnotherapist, who led a guided meditation and discussion group. On Wednesday the Reiki master held her class in alternative healing. Deirdre herself was there two nights a week, Tuesday for a tarot class and Saturday for channeling. She had urged Mariana to take a night, even offered to push one of the other classes to Friday, but Mariana had refused.

"I can't teach anything," Mariana told her.

"Of course you can," Deirdre answered. "You just haven't decided what it is."

Mariana agreed to work three afternoons a week as a psychic reader and to help out with customers in emergencies. Deirdre herself worked three afternoons a week as a reader, the other three doing whatever needed doing. The store was closed on Monday.

A young woman who went by the name Alora Amadea had been a part-time sales clerk for the old owner, and Deirdre had kept her on.

Mariana found Alora's style a bit off-putting—Alora dressed entirely in black, dyed her hair a lifeless shade of that color, wore white makeup, displayed multiple piercings of nose, eyebrows, and ears, and was into ritual magic—but Mariana recognized that the long hours and short pay Deirdre offered were not likely to attract anyone with the skills for a better job. And Alora knew the job, which meant Deirdre didn't have to use her energy hiring and training someone new.

On this day, Alora nodded as Mariana walked into the store, picked up the appointment calendar, and waved it at her.

"Get ready," she said. "You've got a full afternoon."

Mariana took the calendar. Five readings scheduled, two for an hour, three for a half-hour. That left some time open, including a break at two so that she could eat a sandwich and a piece of fruit to maintain her blood sugar level, but she wouldn't have a lot of time to sit around worrying about visions of Brian. Good. She looked at the names. She wasn't often able to connect names with faces, but this time two leapt out at her.

"Alora, we have a challenging situation to deal with this afternoon," she said.

"You mean something sucks," Alora answered.

"Sort of. I have two clients who won't want to run into each other, and who won't be happy to discover that they're both seeing me. Kim at three for half an hour, Pauline at four for an hour. Can you help?"

Mariana handed the calendar back to the young woman.

Alora struck a pose with one hand on her hip, as if she had just been asked to clean the toilet.

"As long as it isn't too busy," she said. "And as long as you're not running late."

Mariana stifled a retort. Arguing with Alora wouldn't be a good way to start the afternoon. "Thank you. I'll try to stay on time. Where's Deirdre?"

"In the stockroom."

Mariana walked down the aisle with the packets of incense on one side and the dishes of small crystals and polished stones on the other, paused to breathe deeply of the heavy mixed scents as she did so, then proceeded to the hall.

Jeff, the hypnotherapist, must have had a heavy session going. Mariana could hear low sobs through the closed door.

The opposite door was open. Mariana checked inside, wanting to say hello to Samantha, but the healer wasn't there.

The next set of doors belonged to the reading room and the stockroom, which was so disorganized that Mariana didn't know how Deirdre could find anything. And she often couldn't.

Mariana heard a file drawer slam.

Deirdre was already elbow-deep into another one when Mariana reached the doorway. Deirdre was short and blonde, with curly hair and smooth, untanned arms, but the long, sleeveless dress with muted purple flowers was something Mariana might have worn. Mariana had a sense that as they worked together, they were starting to resemble each other in an undefinable way.

"I can't find the catalogue," Deirdre said by way of greeting. "The one with the carved wooden Hindu gods. And we need to reorder before the psychic fair."

Deirdre had scheduled a psychic fair, the first since she had bought the store, for the Saturday before Halloween, hoping to bring in new shoppers. It would be Mariana's first psychic fair, and she wasn't looking forward to it. If the fair went well, she would have to read a dozen people in the course of the day, at a discount, with Deirdre taking half the money for the store, rather than her usual twenty-five percent. The thought of twice as many people for half as much money made her brain turn to fuzz.

"I haven't seen the catalogue. And I need a favor," Mariana said.

Deirdre stopped short and looked at her.

"What favor?"

Mariana suppressed a spurt of annoyance. Deirdre had become almost a friend, closer to a friend than anyone else in Mariana's life at the moment, closer than Mariana ever had thought she would be, but her bluntness was still sometimes hard to take. Even harder than Alora's arrogance. It was easier for Mariana to make excuses for Alora.

"Let me know if you can pick up anything about my brother."

"I didn't know you had a brother," Deirdre answered. "I haven't picked one up in your energy field."

"He isn't in my energy field. I don't know where he is."

"But you had a disturbing vision of him, just before you called me this morning," Deirdre said, nodding. "Let's get together for a few minutes at the end of the day. I won't be distracted then."

Mariana left Deirdre to her files and entered the small room, little more than a broom closet, used for psychic readings. The room was furnished only with a round table and two chairs. Mariana had brought in a potted plant, and Deirdre contributed two framed posters with For Sale tags, one of a generic moon goddess and one of frolicking dolphins. Even so, the space was full.

With ten minutes before her first client was due, Mariana had time enough to swish a stick of incense, chant a little, spread her own lacy cloth on the small table, and get a cup of tea. Sometimes her throat got dry, especially when the appointment was for an hour.

"Jenny is here," Alora called.

"Send her back," Mariana answered.

A pudgy woman in her sixties appeared in the doorway.

"My daughter recommended you," Jenny said, a slightly apprehensive smile on her round face. "I've never done this before."

"Come in and sit down," Mariana told her. "And shut the door."

The woman did as she was told.

Mariana felt the hawk settle comfortably on her shoulder.

"Give me your birth date," she said. "I use your birth date to tune in."

Jenny gave her the numbers, and Mariana explained the archetype—the dynamic energy—with which Jenny was attuned, as embodied in the Chariot.

"Your energy is running all over the place, unfocused,"

she said. "You set priorities, but you get too distracted to achieve them."

"Oh, my, yes," the woman agreed.

Then Mariana spread the cards, and the words began to flow from her mouth without difficulty.

"You have a new man in your life," she said, "but you have doubts about the relationship. This has been a time for renewal of joy, and you are getting in the way of your own happiness."

"I haven't even met him, not really," Jenny said, interrupting. "I've only talked to him. On the Internet. And we've exchanged pictures."

"And he's married," Mariana added.

"Yes, but his wife had a stroke."

"And he can't leave her."

The hawk had as much information on the man as Jenny wanted. Even with all Jenny's questions, the time flew by.

Not so her second appointment of the afternoon, a woman in her early fifties, with deep reddish brown hair and pale makeup, named Betty. Betty wanted to know where her soul mate was, and Mariana couldn't see any romantic possibilities in her energy field.

"That's not what the last psychic I saw told me," Betty snapped.

"I can only offer what information I have," Mariana replied.

"Three other psychics have said that my soul mate is in incarnation, and I am on the path to meet him," Betty insisted.

"Then next time you have a reading, it should be with one of those psychics," Mariana said calmly. "And ask why so far they've been wrong."

"You don't understand. They are very good psychics, and they've told me many things that have come true," Betty said.

"One of them especially. This is the only thing she's been wrong about. And she's praying for me, too, special prayers to guide me to my soul mate, but they haven't worked yet. I was supposed to meet him months ago."

"Someone told you that, about your so-called soul mate, and you believed it," Mariana said. "You probably don't even have a soul mate in the way you fantasize. And in the meantime, every moment you spend wondering where he is is a moment that you could be doing something useful."

"Of course I have a soul mate," Betty said, almost gasping for breath. "Everyone does. Plato said that, didn't he? That each of us is only half of a whole, and we need to find the other half?"

Mariana sighed. "Well, he sort of said that. It's in the *Symposium*, which describes a party where several men give their philosophy of love. The one about soul mates is actually kind of a joke. What Socrates says in that dialogue is something different—he talks about what he learned from the priestess Diotima, that the highest form of love is a connection between minds, and that's why we call nonphysical love, ideal love, platonic."

Betty glared at her. Mariana was telling her too much that she didn't want to hear.

"Well, if you don't want to call him a soul mate, that's fine. When do you see me having a lover, a companion, anything?" Betty asked.

"Not in the near future, but of course that can change," Mariana said. She really wanted to say, not in this lifetime. Even more than that, though, she wanted to avoid further argument.

She didn't like arguing with clients, but giving in to them was worse. She was relieved when Betty's half-hour was up.

"I'm going to talk to the psychic who's praying for me,"

Betty said as she was leaving. "I'm going to tell her what you've said."

"And I'm sure she'll tell you what you want to hear," Mariana said.

Betty stalked out. Mariana halfway expected her to ask for her money back, but she didn't.

By the end of the afternoon, Mariana was tired of dealing with other people's problems. But at least everything had gone smoothly—Alora had done her job, making sure that Kim and Pauline didn't intersect. Both women were being visited by the spirit of a man they had been married to, with Kim the mother of his children and Pauline the later trophy wife, and each was receiving messages that she was his one true love.

According to the hawk, both women were right. The man was a philanderer in death as he had been in life. But there was no reason to tell them that, so Mariana didn't. She merely validated their dreams of love.

When her last appointment was over, Mariana took a moment for a mental shower, washing away the energy from the readings. This one was more effective than the one she had tried before leaving home. Then she went to find Deirdre.

Deirdre was behind the counter, busy selling several large and expensive crystals that had become even more expensive once she added her profit. Alora had already left for the day. Mariana waited quietly until the customer paid for her purchases and said good-bye.

Deirdre counted out the money due Mariana for the readings and handed it to her.

"Well?" Mariana asked, as she folded the bills and slipped them into her wallet.

"About your brother? You need to come to one of the channeling sessions," Deirdre told her. "Wherever your brother is, he's shielded. I can't find him. I think he's alive, though. He'd be easier to locate if he weren't. But Baba-ji will have access to more information than I have now."

"I think you're right. I think he's alive." At least she hoped so. "Channeling is the only way you can get more information?"

"Yes."

"All right. I'll come tomorrow night."

Deirdre nodded. "You had a good day today. I hope you have the same tomorrow."

"And a good evening to you."

Mariana didn't really want to come to the channeling session. The first time she had heard Deirdre channeling, a disaster followed—Deirdre's brother had almost been killed in a freak auto accident. She had come twice more to the Saturday night sessions since she and Deirdre had been working together, but she was never really comfortable. Still, the channeling was probably the best approach to finding Brian, or at least confirming that he was somewhere on the planet.

She didn't know what else to do. Not when her guides were so insistently silent where Brian was concerned. Not even in dreams could she find him.

She got into the dark green Mustang that she had inherited when her husband was murdered and drove home.

Miles and Ella were waiting. Mariana fed them, then checked her answering machine. The only message was from Art Freeman, the man she had become involved with after Tim's murder, when her psychic abilities were beginning to demand attention. She didn't know what she could say to him. She decided she didn't need to call back at once.

Besides, she needed to feed herself. She checked the refrigerator for food. Friday meant almost empty shelves, because Saturday was the day of the Farmers Market, the day she shopped. Broccoli and lettuce. And that was about it. A small salad and sauteed broccoli on pasta would have to do.

Mariana took the meal into the bedroom, where the cats were waiting. She had rented a video, a high-budget thriller that probably looked better on a big screen, but was silly enough that she hadn't wanted to waste time, energy, and money to see it in a theater. The three of them spent the evening as they did most evenings — curled up together in bed, watching television until she was sleepy enough to turn it off. Marking time, she thought. So much of her life had become simply marking time.

Under the best of circumstances, Mariana was a light sleeper. She had stopped trying to remember the best of circumstances a long time before. She dozed through the night.

The light was dim, and she couldn't see very far.

She waited for the dragon-prowed ship until the light was entirely gone, and on into the night, but it didn't come.

She curled up on the sand to wait.

Chapter Three

The thin rays of sun that slipped through the slats in the mini-blinds woke Mariana before seven, in plenty of time for a cup of coffee and a shower before her Saturday trip to the Farmers Market.

Wandering among the stalls of fruits, vegetables, and flowers, all glowing with freshness and a kind of vitality that didn't exist in the fluorescent light of supermarkets, was a kind of walking meditation, a way of centering herself that she looked forward to each week.

She even looked forward to the sounds of the three aging cowboys twanging corny old country music on their guitars, something she wouldn't have thought likely.

This day, she hummed along with *The Tennessee Waltz* while poking through the greens, pausing in disappointment when she discovered that there was no fresh basil to be found.

"I should have stocked up," she said to the chunky man in a Dodgers cap who ran one of the organic produce stands.

He nodded. "We'll have some hothouse basil next week, but it isn't quite the same. You'll have to wait until May for the next big bunches."

There was still zucchini, though, and tomatoes, still the stacks of newly picked white corn, still a few flats of the small sweet Seascape strawberries that never made it to the grocery stores because of their limited shelf life. She chose a head of leafy red lettuce, and arugula and baby bok choy, mentally preparing dinner for the next few days.

By the time she got back to her apartment, she had to rush to pack her lunch and get ready to go to the store. Deciding what to wear slowed her a little, but a long gray skirt and a loose white tunic finally made the cut, and she reached Enchantment a few minutes before noon.

Alora greeted her again by waving the appointment calendar. Mariana had to admit as she looked at the girl that wearing black all the time conferred one advantage—never having to think about clothes.

"Six appointments," Alora said. "I left you a break at two."

Saturday was always a busy day for Mariana and a long one for Deirdre, who had the channeling session in the evening.

Mariana looked at the card. The names were all unfamiliar.

"Thanks for remembering to leave a break," she said. There had been days when Alora had forgotten to do that, when Mariana hadn't been able to eat until three, which left her feeling slightly ill, slightly off center, by the time her work was done. Food acted to keep her grounded. She was careful of her choices, though, convinced that the need to feel grounded was why so many psychics overate and got fat.

"Karen is waiting," Alora said, nodding toward a young woman who was checking out earrings.

"I'll be right with you," Mariana told the woman. "Just let me get a cup of tea."

"Okay," Karen said. Her voice was so quiet that Mariana barely heard her.

Mariana waved quickly at Samantha as she walked down the hall to the reading room, not waiting for a hello. Jeff's door was closed. This time there were no sounds.

It took only a moment for Mariana to check the room, set up her cards, and get the cup of tea.

Mariana ushered Karen inside, and they settled into the two chairs.

"I want to show you a picture," Karen said, rummaging in her purse. She found an envelope, then took a wallet-sized photo of a man in a tux and a woman in a wedding gown out of it to hand to Mariana.

The man was handsome, if a little too slick. He wasn't looking at the woman, who was smiling radiantly for the camera. Mariana was startled when she realized that the happy woman in the gown was Karen.

"I want to know if you think he will come back to me," Karen added.

Mariana didn't even need to check with the hawk for that one, although she asked for confirmation.

"Instead of focusing on him," Mariana said, "why don't we look at your choices, at what you want your life to look like."

Karen's eyes started to fill, and Mariana pushed a box of tissues toward her. It was going to be a long afternoon, she could tell.

The next three appointments were also women who needed to consult a psychic about lost love and broken dreams. Mariana's fifth appointment was a musician who had come at his girlfriend's urging—the woman hoped that if a psychic told him to get a day job and give up his fantasies, he might do it. Instead, the hawk gave Mariana a vision of a tour of Europe that she passed on to the young man, his if he didn't give up.

"I'm not giving up," the young man said, laughing in a way that reminded Mariana of her late husband.

"Good," Mariana said. She almost told him that she had once loved a musician, but she rarely offered personal information, and decided not to make an exception.

Her last appointment for the day was again a man. Mariana had taken a short break for a trip to the restroom and a fresh cup of tea, and she returned to the reading room to discover a small man wearing a woolen cap and a jacket too heavy for the day. Most of her clients were women. Two men in one day was a surprise.

Beneath the navy blue wool two small dark eyes looked up at her from the round white face.

"My name is Umberto," he said. "Have you heard of me?"

"No," Mariana replied, "not unless you write long Italian novels."

Umberto laughed. "Good. I'm not Umberto Eco."

Mariana nodded. "I didn't think you were. Does that mean you want a reading?"

"Yes. I was told to come here today and get one."

"Okay. Have a seat, and let's start."

She sent a thought to the hawk, asking what she needed to know about who he was and who sent him. The hawk merely indicated that she should proceed with the reading.

Once Umberto was settled in the chair, Mariana asked for his birth date. He shook his head.

"No help," he said. "Start by describing one of my guides."

Mariana had a spurt of annoyance that he felt the need to test her. She let it go, not wanting it to get in the way of the flow of information. She occasionally saw guides, but not always.

This time she was given the image.

"Male Native American warrior," she said, "with a famous name."

"Very good." Umberto laughed again. "What's his name?"

The image shifted slightly. All she saw was white feathers. She tried to get more, but the white feathers waved at her.

"White Eagle? Is that it? Is White Eagle one of your guides?"

"All right," Umberto said. "Yes. White Eagle is one of my guides. I'll give you my birth date."

Mariana quickly added the numbers. "Your card is the Hermit. You need to be alone."

Umberto wasn't happy with that.

"I don't want to live alone any longer. I want to live with the Foundation. That's why I came today. I want to know if I'll get to live with the Foundation," he said.

"Let's take a look." Mariana spread the cards. She paused to take a sip of tea and assess the patterns in the layout. "Well, something is going to change dramatically for you. And it does have something to do with the Foundation."

"Good. I thought so."

"But I'm not certain you're going to live with them."

"Zelandra thinks I will."

"Is Zelandra the woman with money who is taking care of herself at the expense of others?"

Umberto started to reply, hesitated, then said, "I can see how she would appear that way to you."

"According to the cards, you have an intuitive grasp of your own situation," Mariana said. "You know you're psychic, don't you?"

"Yes, but that doesn't mean I can read for myself. And I don't charge for my services." He looked at her sternly as he said it.

"I understand," Mariana answered, ignoring the look. "Right now you have a choice about your future with important consequences, a choice that it is important for you to make from a spiritual perspective, not a mundane one. And it all has to do with this Foundation. Would you like to check your options? We can do a couple of spreads to illustrate what your life looks like, depending on what choice you make." Mariana liked to do that, even with other psychics, to show people that their choices really made a difference.

"No," Umberto said. "I've already made my choice."

The reading was a difficult one for her because nothing seemed clear. The hawk seemed willing to let White Eagle speak to her directly, but White Eagle didn't seem to want to volunteer much information.

And the cards were cautioning that one possible choice led to disaster. Mariana hoped that wasn't the choice Umberto was making.

She was glad when the afternoon was over.

Deirdre was behind the counter ringing up Umberto's purchases when Mariana was ready to leave.

"See you later," Mariana said.

"Yes. I hope Baba-ji can help about your brother," Deirdre replied.

Home was close enough that Mariana made a quick trip there to feed the cats, returning for Deirdre's channeling session in the evening.

The Saturday night channeling attracted anywhere from three to a dozen people. The classroom was set up with cups, tea bags, and water supply on a table in one corner, and eight chairs in a circle. The three regulars, who could be counted on even if no one else showed up, were in their seats when Mariana arrived.

Lena, a white-haired woman apparently without friends or family who came to almost every class Enchantment offered, was in her usual chair at what would be Deirdre's right when Deirdre was ready to begin. Her round body was disguised by a long, heavy trenchcoat that covered everything down to her shins. The coat looked like one Dan Rather might have worn to file reports on a long-ago foreign war and then sent to the Salvation Army. Lena had helped herself to a cup of herb tea, which she was sipping while waiting for Deirdre.

Next to her sat Bernard and Stella, who were both a little younger than Lena, but not much. The fringe of hair that circled Bernard's shiny bald pate was as white as Lena's. Stella, his wife, was the youngest of the three, a perky sixty-something who still wore jeans and sweatshirts.

Stella waved at Mariana.

"Are you joining us tonight?" she asked.

"In a minute," Mariana replied, backing toward the door. She wasn't certain she wanted to expose her vision of Brian to this group after all. She had forgotten how much Stella loved to hear—and repeat—other people's problems.

But Deirdre was blocking the door.

"Small circle tonight," she said.

"Yes," Mariana said. And with Deirdre there, Mariana wasn't willing to make it smaller by leaving. She took a seat across from Bernard, leaving an empty space between her chair and the one Deirdre would sit in.

Deirdre lit a white candle and a stick of sandalwood incense. She walked the perimeter of the area, chanting softly, before placing the candle on a small table in the corner, with the incense stick in a holder next to it. Then she returned to the circle and sat.

"Sit up straight, chakras aligned," she said, and waited until she was satisfied with everyone's posture. "Now, close your eyes and focus on your breath."

Deirdre led them through a brief meditation on the chakras, the energy centers of the body, then asked them to continue focusing on their breath while she summoned Baba-ji, the entity that spoke through her vocal cords when she went into a light trance.

Mariana watched as Deirdre closed her eyes and focused on her own breathing. She was slightly uncomfortable with the process by which Deirdre turned her body over to another, but Deirdre did it easily enough. Within seconds, she was ready to begin.

"Good evening, dear ones," Deirdre said, eyes closed, voice lower, "and welcome. I am glad you could come to our regular meeting. How may I be of service this evening?"

"I still feel that I don't know my life's mission, Baba-ji," Lena said. "Please tell me what I'm supposed to be doing."

Mariana tuned out the answer. Lena always asked about her life's mission, and Baba-ji always told her to keep meditating and the answer would be revealed to her. Baba-ji had tried being more specific, but Lena didn't seem to hear. Even ascended masters sometimes failed to communicate.

"No questions, Baba-ji," Bernard said, when it was his turn.

Bernard never had any questions.

"I have a question, Baba-ji," Stella said. "My son has a new girlfriend, and she is so cold and mean and calculating I think she must have reptilian DNA. Is my son dating a reptile?"

Deirdre was quiet. Baba-ji was evidently weighing the reply. Mariana was curious about this one.

"Your son is dating a woman whose heart is closed," Deirdre's lowered voice finally said. "But her DNA, as you put it, is of the same species as your own."

"Are you sure, Baba-ji? I know they've been interbreeding with us in an attempt to save their own species. I still remember how chilled I was, when they abducted me, and I am so grateful that I was past my breeding prime so they didn't try to impregnate me, but I do think this woman's eyes remind me of the ones I saw that night." Stella was off and running.

Mariana closed her eyes and waited for silence. She half-way believed in UFOs, mostly because she couldn't believe that Earth was the only populated planet, and she supposed it was possible that a reptilian life form from outer space was trying to take over the world by interbreeding with humans, but it sounded like something from a television miniseries.

In fact, it had been a television miniseries. When Mariana once pointed this out to Stella, Stella told her that television sometimes got it right, and the show was able to air only because the reptilian plan to take over all media hadn't yet succeeded.

Mariana was startled when the silence came, when she opened her eyes and realized that Lena, Bernard, and Stella were all waiting for her to ask a question.

"Yes, dear one?" Deirdre's voice prompted.

"I had a vision of my brother yesterday, Baba-ji," Mariana said. "I would like to know if he is still alive, and if there is some way I can contact him."

"You and the entity who is your brother have been close for many lives, so close that in this life you inhabited your mother's womb together. And you are still close in spirit, and another way, even though you have not seen him or heard from him in what seems to you a long time."

"It is a long time," Mariana said. Lena frowned at her for interrupting, but she persisted. "How are we still close?"

"Your brother is not far from where you live, within an hour's drive. And this day has provided you a contact with an entity who can help you find him. I wish you well on your journey. Are there other questions?"

"Yes, Baba-ji," Lena said. "I wondered if you would help me with a dream. I was in a room in a strange house, and I couldn't find the light switch, but I could almost see in the dark."

Mariana almost cut Lena off to say that her question hadn't really been answered. She knew, though, that Baba-ji's abruptness meant that he had told her as much about Brian as he was going to this evening. Wishing her luck on the journey was spirit-speak for telling her that there were some things she would have to discover for herself.

If she had made a contact earlier in the day that would help her, it had to be one of the readings. One of the love-struck women, the musician, or the strange Umberto. Umberto was the most likely. She hoped he had paid by check, so she could get a telephone number. And she hoped he wouldn't mind a surprise phone call.

She waited restlessly through Lena's dreams and Stella's conspiracy theories, marveling at Baba-ji's patience, and understanding why Deirdre might want to leave her body rather than listen to the same stuff—she wouldn't quite call it drivel —week after week. She also understood that Deirdre needed the money.

Baba-ji finally left, and Deirdre's face and voice returned to normal. She smiled at the small group.

"That's all for tonight," she said. "I hope this has been helpful."

Lena and Stella assured her that it had been. Bernard stood, ready to leave. Mariana stood, too.

"I'll wait for you in front," she called over the two older women's heads.

Deirdre nodded.

A door from the classroom led to an alley with parking spaces, but Mariana had parked her car in one of the spaces in front of the store. She walked down the hall to the retail area, knowing Deirdre would have to come that way to turn off the last of the lights and set the alarm.

The overhead lights had been turned off and the bolt had

been thrown on the front door before the channeling began to keep stragglers away from the merchandise. A sign directed latecomers to the alley. Mariana took the sign down and put it behind the counter.

She knew that Deirdre had put the day's receipts in an envelope, ready for a night deposit at the bank, and she needed to get the phone number. If there was one—if Umberto had paid by check.

Her glance returned to the glass front door, where something didn't look quite right. There was a dark form huddled against it. She unbolted the door and pushed. The form didn't move. The streetlight was too far away to give her any sense of the lump's contents.

She was still pushing when Deirdre showed up.

"What's wrong?" Deirdre asked.

"Help me," Mariana replied. "Hold the door so I can get this thing out of the way."

Deirdre put her weight against the door, allowing it to stay open a few inches, while Mariana grabbed at what turned out to be a dark jacket and a man's body.

The body finally rolled to one side.

Her hand came away wet.

"Turn on the lights," she said.

Deirdre swung the door open and moved to the light switch.

The wetness on Mariana's hand was blood.

And the body under the dark jacket was covered with it.

In a moment of terror, she thought the body might be Brian's, that her vision of the morning before was coming true, but the body wasn't his, she knew that.

She didn't have to look at the features under the wool cap.

She already knew that it was the round white face of Umberto, and that whatever choice he made that afternoon had indeed led him to disaster.

As the dragon-prowed ship sailed across the ocean, strange things were happening to her body, more than just a gender change. She became male and old and light and somehow elongated.

The shore he stepped onto was so bright that it looked painted. The trees and the flowers and the rocks were too sharply defined to be real.

He was wearing a long robe and sandals and a high pointed hat.

A fairy was fluttering at his feet, gasping for help.

But his wand was useless.

The fairies were dying, and his wand was useless.

He wanted to get back on the ship, but he lived there in the painted land a long time after the fairies died, a long time before he could leave and return to the land on the other side of the ocean.

She felt a surge of relief, and guilt, when she finally looked down to see that the bare feet on the sand were her own.

Chapter Four

"We have to call the police," Mariana said, shivering. She stared at her hand, uncertain what to do about the blood.

"Wash it off," Deirdre said, responding first to Mariana's unasked question. "I'll call them."

Cradling her hand as if it were cut, Mariana retreated to the tiny room that held a toilet, wash basin, and a narrow shelf for supplies. She turned the water on and hit the plunger on the soap dispenser. Her hand foamed bright red, then the color softened. She watched the pink water run down the drain.

When she returned to the front of the store, Deirdre was standing near the door, watching the parking lot.

"Are you picking up anything?" Mariana asked.

"Only our own fear."

"Yes. Me too."

They stood in silence after that, waiting.

The paramedics were the first to arrive, two young men, followed shortly by two uniformed officers, a man and a woman, in a black-and-white. The four of them conferred briefly.

The paramedics moved Umberto just enough so that the officers could enter the store.

"Did you know the man?" the female officer asked.

"He was here this afternoon," Mariana said. "Did he

bleed to death? What happened to him?"

The officer nodded. "Someone stabbed him through the heart. Marks on his face and his wrists indicate that he was bound and gagged. There isn't a lot of blood around, so we think he was stabbed somewhere else and his body brought here." She paused to assess the two women's reactions, then continued. "His wallet is missing. We were hoping you could identify him."

"I'm not sure how much we can help." Mariana turned to Deirdre. "I meant to ask earlier—did he write a check?"

Deirdre moved behind the counter and pulled the zippered bag with the day's receipts out of a drawer beneath the cash register.

"What was his name?" she asked.

"Umberto. That's all he told me," Mariana replied.

Deirdre leafed through the checks and the credit card receipts and shook her head.

"He must have paid cash," she said.

"What about the appointment calendar?" Mariana asked. "Maybe Alora got his phone number."

The calendar was on the counter, next to the phone. Deirdre glanced at it, and this time she nodded.

"We do have a phone number, but no last name," she said. She reached for a pad, copied the information, and handed the slip of paper to the officer.

Mariana glanced at the number and shut her eyes, hoping she could hold it in her memory until she had a chance to write it down. Perhaps Umberto wasn't the contact who would lead her to her brother. Perhaps someone else at that number was.

"What did he have an appointment for?" the officer asked, looking from Deirdre to Mariana.

"A reading," Mariana said, feeling herself starting to

blush. "I'm a psychic."

The female officer struggled to maintain her composure. Her partner lost his.

"And you didn't tell him he was going to get stabbed to death?" He was laughing so hard that Mariana barely understood the words.

"This is not a science," Deirdre began, but Mariana held up a hand to stop her.

"I told him there was a possible disaster ahead, and whether it happened depended on a choice he had to make. That was the best I could do." Her heart was beating rapidly, and she worked to control her breathing, trying to reduce the flush on her face.

"Okay." The male officer shook his head. "The detectives will be here any minute, and I know they'll want to talk with you."

"Okay," Mariana echoed. "I'm going to make a cup of tea. Would anyone else like one?"

Both officers declined. Deirdre followed Mariana down the hall to the classroom.

"This isn't your fault," she said.

"I know that. Keep telling me anyway," Mariana answered.

She tore the foil wrapper from a lemon ginger tea bag, dropped it in a paper cup, then filled the cup from the red tap of the heavy stand that held the bottled spring water. She remembered to hold the cup carefully, fighting the urge to scald the place where Umberto's blood had covered her skin.

"Being a psychic, tuning into the energy flows of the future, is an art," Deirdre said. "And nothing is certain until it happens. If you told him that one path led to disaster, you gave the warning you were supposed to give."

"Thanks. And how do I explain that to the police?"

"I don't see why you have to. And if you continue to worry this much about what the mundane world thinks of you, you'll never make it as a professional psychic." Deirdre smiled, but not enough to take the sting out of the words.

Mariana opened her mouth to argue, then shut it again. This wasn't the time. Besides, Deirdre might be right.

"Just answer their questions," Deirdre added. "And remember that it's about Umberto, not about you."

"All right. Let's go."

Mariana dropped her tea bag in the trashcan and started toward the front, too annoyed to acknowledge that Deirdre had done her a favor with the verbal slap.

Two men, one wearing jeans and a brown leather bomber jacket over a plaid shirt, the other wearing an open-necked white shirt with navy blue sport coat and khakis, had joined the uniformed officers inside the store. Outside, other men had joined the paramedics. Someone was taking pictures.

Mariana focused on the detectives. The one in jeans had gray hair and a mustache and a face that seemed a little puffy, as if he hadn't had enough sleep. The one in the white shirt was younger, dark-haired and clean-shaven, with olive skin.

"I'm Detective Claybourne," the jeans-clad one said, flashing a badge. "And this is my partner, Detective Torres. Which one of you owns the store?"

"I do," Deirdre said.

"And you are?" The detective turned to Mariana.

"Mariana Morgan. I work here three afternoons a week."

"As a psychic." He said it with a straight face, and Mariana didn't blush. "What were you doing here tonight?"

"We had a small group meeting in the back," Deirdre answered. "I was channeling. Mariana came, and so did three other people."

"But not the person—Umberto—you found by the front door?"

"No." This time Mariana spoke up before Deirdre could answer. "He had a one-hour appointment with me this afternoon, and I didn't see him after that until we came back out here."

"Was he a regular client?"

"No. I'd never seen him before."

"Neither had I," Deirdre added.

"Okay. You said there were three other people. Can you give me their names and a way to get in touch with them?"

"Yes. They're regular customers," Deirdre said, reaching for the Rolodex that sat next to the phone.

"How did they leave?" the detective asked.

"There's a back door," Deirdre said. "They left directly from the classroom."

"May I see?"

"I'll take you," Mariana said. She volunteered because she was too edgy to stand there waiting.

The detective followed her down the aisle between the incense and crystals and into the hall.

"Tell me about this appointment," he said.

Mariana hesitated, then opened the door to the reading room and flicked on the lights.

"This is my office," she said, gesturing toward the table and chairs. "I mostly read tarot, but I pass on channeled information as well. I'll tell you what I remember of the hour, but I don't remember much of it. I see one or two people on a slow day, six today, and I don't save the details in my long-term memory."

"I bet you could remember some of this one if you thought about it. From your short-term memory." The detective smiled. He looked younger when he smiled, as if the gray hair might have been premature. "You know, I tried working with a psychic for a while. I'd give her photographs, and she'd give me information. I was always amazed at what she could come up with by looking at a photograph. She was pretty accurate. The only problem was that none of the information ever helped me break a case."

Mariana smiled back. "And here you are trying to get information from two of us."

"Well, my partner can deal with your friend."

"Okay. I remember that Umberto challenged me to come up with the name of his guide—White Eagle. He had psychic abilities of his own, although he didn't charge for using them and didn't seem to think that I should. And there was something about wanting to live with the Foundation, whatever that is, and a woman with a strange name. I'll let you know if I remember her name. But that's it." She turned off the lights and shut the door.

"Nothing about being killed, I suppose."

At least he said it with a straight face.

"No. Nothing about being killed." Mariana felt a twinge of guilt as she said it, wishing she could have given Umberto a warning. In a sense, though, she had. "I remember telling him that he had a choice to make, and one path led to a disaster. Although I probably didn't use that word. Psychics don't like to talk about possible disasters. I usually just call it a challenge." Mariana smiled, hoping the detective would as well.

He did. "Yeah, it was that."

Mariana moved away from the door, intending to lead him on to the classroom, but he blocked her way. The detective was a big man, with broad shoulders and a slight paunch, as if he had been an athlete but was now losing his muscle tone.

"There must have been more," he said.

"Of course, he was here for an hour." She started blushing

again. "I just don't remember it right now. I'll see what I can come up with later."

"Okay." He turned to let her pass. "And I want to hear everything you come up with, about the Foundation and the woman with the strange name, even if it wasn't something that was actually said in the session."

This time she looked at his eyes, which were light greenish-brown. Hazel, she thought. And familiar. She wondered why his eyes were familiar.

"The classroom is this way," she said.

He didn't spend much time looking around after verifying that the back door led to an alley and that it was now locked.

This time Mariana blocked the hall.

"If the psychic you worked with wasn't helpful, what makes you think I might be?" she asked.

"Maybe you won't be," Claybourne replied. "Maybe this is random violence. But there are a couple of reasons I don't think so. The first is that the body was dumped on your doorstep. The second is that he was apparently stabbed with some kind of crystal. It's still imbedded in the wound. So I need the information, whatever information you can give."

"Stabbed with a crystal?"

Claybourne nodded. "Or at least that's what it looks like. We'll have to take a closer look later."

"Who would stab someone with a crystal?" Mariana asked. When Claybourne just shook his head, she added, "Do you think we might be in danger?"

"Do you?"

Mariana laughed nervously. "I can't tune in. Neither can Deirdre, not right now. We just pick up each other's fear, something like what happens in an echo chamber."

Claybourne nodded. "If you like, we can give you a ride home."

"I'm not that afraid. I'm not really afraid for myself. But I don't know how to focus on a bloody body without feeling the fear."

"Most people don't. And it's not something you want to learn."

Mariana nodded. "You're right. Is there anything else you need to know about the store?"

"Not tonight. We'll be in touch."

She led him back to the front room. Deirdre was standing in front of the counter, alone. She had picked up her carryall and wrapped herself in a blue and purple paisley shawl.

"I have to get home," she said. "The babysitter has to leave."

"Okay," Detective Claybourne said. "I don't see any reason why you can't go ahead and lock up the store."

He looked at each of them and added, "Remember to call me if you come up with anything you think I should know."

"Okay." Mariana said, nodding, wanting it to be okay, not really believing that it was.

The detective nodded back. She watched him leave, join the group of people still clustered outside the front door.

"He's married," Deirdre said.

"What?"

"That detective. He's married. He's wearing a ring."

"Who said I care?"

"You made some kind of connection with him," Deirdre said. "There's a link between the two of you."

"I know. I recognized his eyes," Mariana said. "But that doesn't mean the link is anything other than professional. Baba-ji said that a contact I made today would help me find my brother. His words were a little ambiguous. I thought he meant this afternoon, but maybe he meant this evening. Maybe the contact is the detective."

"Maybe." Deirdre placed her carryall on the counter. She

took a stick of incense from a drawer beneath the cash register and lit it. "I really do have to get out of here. But I think we need to do a little cleansing first. Come with me."

The two women walked from room to room, Deirdre waving the incense, Mariana clapping her hands.

In each room they chanted, "Only creatures of the Light are welcome here. Any creature not of the Light must leave. If you wish to be lifted up, we ask that you be lifted up. But you must leave now."

They ended up back at the front door.

Deirdre set the incense stick upright in a bowl of sand so that it could burn to the end after they left.

"I'll have to do it again tomorrow," she said. "With sage and a bell. By then I should be able to sense whether there is anything hanging around. Samantha will do another cleansing with Reiki when she gets here, unless you want to do that now."

"No. She's more accomplished than I am, and I want to leave. I'll see you Thursday," Mariana said. "Call me if you need anything before then."

Deirdre turned out the main lights, leaving only a small night light at the front door.

"Goodnight, Mariana," she said.

Mariana opened the door and felt momentarily assaulted by the energies of the group still checking the crime scene.

Umberto's body was gone. She was glad Umberto's body was gone.

Detective Claybourne waved at her, and she waved back, but she headed straight to her car without pausing, without saying goodnight.

She was glad to get home to her cats. And she was surprised to discover she was so exhausted that she fell asleep almost as soon as she made it to her bed.

56

The ship with the dragon prow took her to a wine dark sea. Her skin became mahogany, and her gown became a draped white toga. The jewelry around her neck and on her arms was heavy and gold, weighing her down like chains.

The dragon prow disappeared. The ship became longer, growing multiple banks of oars and men who held them, working under a man with a whip.

The man who stood beside her wore a breastplate and a skirt made of leather strips. His eyes were the color of the water.

She knew she belonged to him. If it were not for her rage at this, she might have loved him.

They landed, and then they were at a villa, where she lived almost comfortably in slave quarters. A gilded cage.

He could have freed her, but he refused. He kept her as he kept the pair of young leopards that he had trained to a leash. There was always the chance the leopards might turn on him, but they didn't.

She thought of poisoning him. But she didn't.

One day he went to sea and didn't come back.

She was sold to an old man, and that night she opened her veins.

Her spirit floated back to the dragon-prowed ship, where it found her new body. The ship returned her to the sands from which she started.

The sadness stayed, and the memory of his eyes.

Who . . .

Chapter Five

Mariana waited until Monday before calling Claybourne. She had spent an hour on Sunday meditating, focusing on her appointment with Umberto, hoping to come up with something that would be useful to the police. And she had finally been given the name of the woman.

"Zelandra," Mariana told him. "The woman's name was Zelandra. I told Umberto that she was taking care of herself at the expense of those around her."

"Can you spell Zelandra?" Claybourne asked.

"Only if it's just like it sounds. Did you find out anything from the telephone number?"

"Not much. The number gave us Umberto's last name—Marconi—and an address in Oxnard, in kind of a rundown area. The landlord didn't have much information on him, just that he lived alone. Quietly. We'll start going through his things today, but that'll take a while. His car was left in the parking lot in front of Enchantment, and we may get some information from that, too." Claybourne hesitated, then added, "The body was dumped at your door as some kind of message, you know that, don't you?"

"I'm not sure I know that, but I'll think about it."

"Okay. Do you have any idea what he did for a living?"

"No." Mariana shut her eyes, hoping for some help. None came. "I think I told you, he had psychic abilities, but he said

58

he didn't charge for his services. I had the sense that he was concerned about money, though. And he said he didn't want to live alone any longer. He wanted to live with Zelandra and the Foundation. That's really all I remember."

"And you don't have any idea where either the woman or the Foundation might be." The detective sounded disappointed.

"I'm afraid not. But I do have a sense that she's nearby. I have a sense of her energy from the reading with Umberto. I'll let you know if anything becomes clearer." Mariana paused for breath. "Could I ask you about something else?"

"Sure."

"If you were me, and you wanted to find someone, and your guides wouldn't help, what would you do?"

"I'd try the Internet."

The answer caught Mariana off guard. She had to laugh.

"Of course. Everything you can possibly want is on the Internet, isn't it?"

"And a lot of things you don't want," Claybourne said.

"But I'd have to have some kind of information to start with, wouldn't I?"

"Obvious info like Social Security number or last known address would make it easier. Who are you looking for?"

"My brother."

The pause before the detective answered was so long that Mariana almost filled it.

"I'm sorry," he finally said.

"Not your fault."

"What's your brother's name?"

"Brian. Brian Field."

"Middle name?"

"Edward."

"When I have a minute, I'll check the computer, see if we

have any information on him."

"Thank you. And I'll let you know if I receive any more information on Umberto."

Mariana hung up the phone and moved to her pink meditation chair. What did she know about Brian that could help her find him on the Internet? No Social Security number, no address for years. His last name, Field, the name that had once been hers as well, was a common one. And that was if he had kept it. If he truly wanted to hide, he might not be Brian Edward Field any longer.

But Baba-ji had said that Brian was within an hour's drive. That meant approximately Malibu to the south, Lompoc to the north, and Van Nuys to the east. With many points in between.

Mariana decided that she would be better off going to the library and checking local telephone directories than playing around on the Internet. Sitting while websites downloaded always made her slightly crazy. She just wasn't at ease with the technology. Her other choice for the afternoon was to clean the apartment and do the laundry. The library was more inviting.

Ella had settled onto her lap. Mariana picked up the cat, ignored her protests, and resettled her onto the chair.

The Main Street branch of the library was only a mile and a half away, the sky was clear, the temperature in the high sixties, and Mariana could have walked. Having decided on a course of action, however, she needed to start immediately.

So she drove the Mustang the short distance to the library.

The building had recently been painted a rich green, and the glass entrance refinished with strips of primary colors embedded with literary quotations, an attempt at art that hadn't quite come out right in Mariana's opinion.

Inside, however, the library was quiet and spacious and

comforting. A plump woman with curly white hair and bright red lipstick sat behind the Information/Check Out desk. She nodded at Mariana with the serenity of a volunteer who has no need to look busy.

The man behind the Reference desk stared at a computer screen through the middle of his trifocals. That, plus his shaggy gray hair and frayed polo shirt, marked him as a paid member of the library staff.

Two teenaged boys at the public computers seemed to be the only other patrons in the library.

Mariana walked past them to the reference stacks. The watercolors displayed on the walls, a local artist's work, made up for the strange front doors.

All the telephone directories she could have hoped for were there. She started with Malibu, deciding to work her way up geographically, south to north.

An hour later, she was ready to give up. Brian Field wasn't listed in any of the directories she looked in, even taking some liberties with Baba-ji's sense of driving time.

On impulse, not wanting the trip to be a total waste, she checked Oxnard for Umberto Marconi. The address was there, and the telephone number that he had given at the store. Of course, she could have checked Oxnard addresses from home. But she hadn't been thinking about Umberto then.

Oxnard wasn't that far. She could find the street on a map, take a short trip to Oxnard, and maybe pick up some kind of vibration from the building.

She put the directory back and left the library.

Because she hadn't lived in Ventura long enough to feel comfortable finding places on her own, Mariana kept a Ventura County map in her glove compartment. Oxnard was one of the areas shown in detail.

The street she was looking for wasn't in the city itself. It was in an area known as the Keys, off Harbor Boulevard.

Mariana backtracked along Main Street to Seaward Avenue, where she turned right toward Harbor. She liked to drive down Seaward to the beach sometimes, especially on slightly cloudy days, so that she could chant without worrying whether anyone thought her slightly mad.

This time she turned left on Harbor just after she passed the freeway, driving parallel to the ocean. Mariana had to shut her eyes to all of the signs around the freeway and Harbor Boulevard that told her the directions in terms of the compass. The various norths, souths, easts, and wests simply disoriented her.

For too much of her life, the ocean had been toward the west. Now she had trouble accepting that the ocean might be toward the south because of the curve in the California coastline. So she thought in terms of right or left turns, toward the mountains or toward the ocean, and occasionally watched the sun rise in what felt to her as if it should be the southeast and set in what felt as if it should be the northwest.

Harbor Boulevard took Mariana out of the city and into open fields with signs promising fresh fruits and vegetables at roadside stands. If she ever missed the Farmers Market, she would have to give one of them a try. Ventura County had rigid laws protecting farmland and limiting urban growth. Even knowing that, Mariana was surprised that so much real estate so close to the ocean was planted with acres of strawberries and broccoli.

A massive electrical power facility was also planted in the fields. Mariana could almost feel herself being zapped by emanating electromagnetic waves as she drove by. It couldn't be good to work there.

The cultivated fields gave way to wetlands, a brief patch of unexpected wilderness.

A small liquor store was the signal that she was back in civilization and approaching the Keys. She turned right on Wooley and quickly discovered what Claybourne meant by a rundown area. The packed-together houses looked as if they had been painted once, when first built some fifty years ago, and none had seen a fresh coat of paint since.

Two more turns took her to the address she was looking for. While most of the buildings were single-family dwellings, this was a triplex. Three matching doors, three matching windows with the drapes closed, all framed in cracked beige stucco. Umberto had lived in the center unit.

A police seal on the door warned that no one was allowed to enter.

Mariana stepped up onto the porch. The cement area stretched across the front of the unit, with enough space for a chair and table. Umberto's chair was metal, with peeling white paint. The table was white plastic. The porch to the right sported a jade plant, the one to the left a potted palm. Umberto had evidently decided that the small patches of lawn between walkways provided enough greenery. If he had even noticed.

The chair was dusty, but Mariana sat in it anyway, turning it so that it faced the unit. Her jeans could go in with the rest of the laundry, which would still be waiting when she got home.

She closed her eyes and did her best to quiet her mind.

A clogged drainpipe. That was the image that came to her. Claybourne had said it was going to take a while to go through Umberto's things. Umberto had been a packrat. No wonder he had wanted to move. The apartment was so full of stuff—mostly dirty stuff—that the energy couldn't flow.

And dark. The unit was dark. Even if the drapes had been

open, the unit would still have been dark.

She asked the hawk if Umberto's spirit was anywhere around.

The hawk answered that it was not.

Is there a way I can get information from him, Mariana thought.

The hawk was silent.

"There's no point in waiting for Bert. He isn't coming back."

The voice, a human voice, startled Mariana. She opened her eyes and lost her images.

A woman in her late fifties was standing on the porch that held the jade plant. She had coarse, unruly, gray hair and a lumpy face that included a large mole on her chin. Her dress was so faded that it was impossible to determine the original color or pattern.

"I know he isn't coming back," Mariana said. "I found the body."

The woman's eyes were deeply embedded in fleshy mounds. She struggled to open them wide enough to express shock, and Mariana got a glimpse of irises as faded as the housedress.

"You found him?"

"Yes. I'm sorry. I didn't mean to upset you." That was only partly true. Mariana was annoyed that the woman had interrupted her. But the woman didn't appear to be leaving. "Did you know him well?"

"No. I lived next door to him here for almost ten years, but we both pretty much kept to ourselves. Bert was quiet, that's good when you live this close together."

"You knew him as Bert?"

"I called him that. He didn't mind. How did he die? I heard murder."

"Someone stabbed him and then dropped his body in

front of the store where I work. His body was blocking the door when I tried to leave Saturday night."

The woman shook her head. "Who would do that?"

"I don't know. Did you know any of his friends?"

"No, nor any of his enemies. We didn't talk except to say hello in passing."

"Do you know what he did for a living?"

The woman shook her head again. "I think he worked for the county. But he was psychic, you know. He had visions and things."

A car door slammed, and the woman turned to look. Mariana turned as well and saw Claybourne getting out of an unmarked light blue sedan. Torres was with him. A black-and-white was pulling in behind them.

Claybourne waved to her. "Want to see the inside, as long as you're here?"

"Sure. Why not?"

"Communing with the spirits?" he asked, as he stepped onto the porch.

He was wearing jeans again, with the leather jacket. Torres was again in sport coat and khakis.

The two officers in uniform were male and female, but a different pair from the ones Mariana had met at the store. They each had an armload of flat cardboard, the kind that un-folds into boxes.

"No, I was speaking with—" Mariana turned to introduce the neighbor, but she had left the porch. "I was speaking with Umberto's neighbor. I guess she didn't want to talk with you."

"A neighbor?" Claybourne raised his eyebrows.

His face wasn't as puffy. He must have gotten some sleep over the weekend. And his eyes still reminded Mariana of someone, something. She knew his eyes.

"Yes. She was on the porch. Didn't you see her?"

"No. The landlord told us that a young couple lives there, and both of them work during the day. No one answered when we knocked yesterday." He detoured to the porch with the jade plant and rapped his knuckles forcefully on the door. The unit was silent. "Are you sure you weren't communing with a spirit?"

"She was flesh and blood. She went inside when you got out of the car. You must have scared her."

"You must be joking!" The words came from the uniformed female officer.

"That's right. Tell her I'm a gentle soul," Claybourne said.

"Not about you—about this. Look."

Torres had unsealed the door of Umberto's unit. The female officer was pointing inside.

Mariana stood up and moved closer to the officer to see what she was pointing at.

The mess. She was pointing at the mess.

Torres, who had at some point pulled on plastic gloves, reached inside and flicked a light switch. The light didn't help.

From what Mariana could see, the unit consisted of a living/dining area separated by a counter from a small kitchen. Stairs led up to a loft that was intended for a sleeping area. From where she stood, a bed wasn't visible.

Everything was covered with trash. Sofa, chairs, table, carpet—everything was strewn with clothes, towels, rags, papers, boxes that had once contained gadgets of some sort, and partly eaten food.

The place was not only dirty, it smelled.

"I'm not so sure I want to go in after all," Mariana said, turning to Claybourne. The porch was too crowded, and she found herself too close to him. She stepped back.

"Okay," Claybourne said. "We have to, but you don't."

66

"I just don't think it would help." Her stomach was churning from the odor. And something about the place didn't feel right. Still walking backward, she edged off the porch, preparing to leave. "The woman thought Umberto worked for the county. She called him Bert."

"Comic books." The female officer had stepped inside but was now back in the doorway. "The stacks of papers are old comic books."

"Handle them carefully," Claybourne told her. "They may be worth a lot of money. And someone may come forward to claim them. That's one way of finding a relative."

"Are you going to advertise?" Mariana asked.

"No. Some reporter will do it for us. And we'll check with the county, see if he really did work there. Thanks."

"You're welcome. I'm sorry I can't go in."

"Not a problem." The detective regarded her through dark blue eyes. "I checked the computer. Brian Edward Field doesn't have a police record or a California driver's license. Have you started your Internet search?"

"Not exactly. Baba-ji—he's an enlightened master, Deirdre channels him—said Brian was within an hour's drive. I checked telephone directories instead. That's how I ended up here." Mariana had edged another step away from the door. She was torn between talking with the detective and leaving. "Was he really stabbed with the crystal?"

"In a way. It was pounded into his heart."

Mariana shuddered. "How terrible."

"Would showing it to you help?"

Mariana wanted to say yes, but she knew she couldn't look at it, or at least not then.

"I don't think so," she said.

"Okay. Let me know if you change your mind." Claybourne turned away.

Mariana watched him join the others inside the apartment and shut the door. She wasn't happy about leaving them there. She asked the hawk if they were in any danger. The hawk let her know that they were not. The hawk confirmed that it would not be good for her to go in.

But wouldn't tell her why, or what her next step should be.

Sometimes she just had to wait, she knew that. She accepted the silence and drove home.

As she climbed the stairs to her apartment, Ella began to scream, partly a complaint about having been left alone, partly an insistence on immediate attention once Mariana was inside.

Miles was waiting quietly and confidently in the kitchen.

"You have food," she told them both. But she gave them a little more, just to remind them that she did indeed love them, then went into her combination living room and office to check her answering machine.

The red light blinked.

"It's Art Freeman," a familiar voice told her. "I've been thinking about you, and we need to talk. Please."

Art Freeman again. She had been ignoring his messages for days now, even as his voice had a note of increasing urgency.

Their relationship had crumbled under the pressure of the changes Mariana had been going through. She had been sorry about the breakup, and a little fearful. If she couldn't get along with Art, a man who was sympathetic and open-minded where her unusual talents were concerned, she had to consider the possibility that she couldn't get along with anyone.

Mariana erased the message. He might think they needed to talk, but she wasn't sure. She decided to ask for a dream, for clarity, and make up her mind in the morning.

The dragon-prowed ship was waiting when she arrived at the beach, as if someone on board knew she would be coming.

The trip was a short one. When she disembarked, only her clothing had changed. Her bodice was cut low, baring the upper part of her breasts, and her ruffled skirt was hiked up on one side to expose her leg.

She could hear music, and she wanted to dance.

Two steps took her to the stage, where she joined the other dancers.

The women's faces were blurred, but she knew the men, the one playing piano, the one playing guitar, and the one drinking at the bar. She loved two of them. The third wanted her.

The two she loved were both dead, and the one who wanted her had her, before she was allowed to return to the ship.

When she was back on the shore of her current life, she ran from the beach. But she couldn't outrun her fear.

Who . . .

Chapter Six

Mariana's dreams didn't bring clarity. She knew that Art was in them, and she remembered enough of the images to understand that there was still a tie between them. Not that she felt the tie in her normal waking mode. Days would go by when she didn't think about him unless he called and left a message.

Art's words had expressed urgency, his voice discomfort. It was possible his discomfort came simply from the fact that they hadn't talked in months, not since she had ended their affair. Mariana suspected, however—and the hawk agreed— that his discomfort was deeper. He wanted to stop thinking about her, and he hadn't been able to do it. That would even explain the growing urgency, but the hawk was silent about the urgency.

She could tap into memories of moments of joy with him. If she wasn't careful, though, the tap skewed into the terror in her life that had surrounded the beginning of the relationship. She didn't blame that on Art. She just didn't want to see him anymore.

But she called him anyway, waiting until evening, when he would be home from work.

"Something is wrong," he said. "I'm afraid something is going to happen to you."

Mariana hesitated before answering. "I don't think that has anything to do with me," she finally said. "Is it possible that your desire to see me turned to a fear that something would happen to me? That you came up with this because you needed a reason to call me?"

"I don't think so. I don't know. I do want to see you. I won't even try to lie to you," he said. "I ache when I remember you. I want to see you again. Please."

"How would that help?" she asked. His pain was so powerful that it vibrated in her hand as she held the telephone receiver. "I'm not willing to start anything, you know that."

"I don't know if it would help. But maybe I could convince you to change your mind. And maybe you are in danger, maybe I really have tuned in to something."

Mariana closed her eyes, again searching for the right answer. "I won't change my mind. And I don't think I'm in danger. I suspect that you're starting to develop your own psychic ability, and right now it isn't focused. But if you'd like to drive out here for lunch, we could do that on Sunday."

"Is that the best you'll offer?" The disappointment was as clear as the pain had been. "Why not dinner Friday?"

"Okay." The word was out before Mariana could stop it. "Dinner Friday."

She gave him directions to the apartment and hung up.

She wanted to release his pain, the pain that she hadn't intended to absorb and hadn't been able to stop when it flowed through the telephone wires. The only way she could think to do it was through a long walk, but the sun had set, and she didn't like to walk at night.

"I need to do a better job of protecting myself from other people's pain," she said aloud.

The hawk silently agreed.

In truth, she had offered the lunch date partly because it was the only thing she could do for him and partly because the situation with Art was the only dilemma in her life that she felt she had any control over. She had agreed to dinner because she didn't want to argue. And thus had lost control of the situation after all.

Her dreams hadn't provided any new information about either Brian's whereabouts or Umberto's murder. She fretted without focus, not sure what she should do next about either one.

If Brian wanted to be found, he would be. If he didn't want to be found, part of her was as reluctant to force herself on him as another part of her was anxious to reestablish contact. An impasse.

The circumstances of Umberto's death had marked Mariana as somehow involved. And the more she feared she might be involved, the less the hawk would tell her. Another impasse.

She decided to set everything aside until Thursday, when she could discuss it with Deirdre.

"A hot bath and a good night's sleep," she said to the cats. "Tomorrow, meditation and exercise, and Thursday, back to work."

Miles seemed to think that was a good idea. Ella was already asleep on the pink meditation chair.

The plan sounded better in theory than it played out. Wednesday crawled by. Her meditation felt empty and fruitless, and her exercise more tiring than refreshing.

By Thursday morning, Mariana was more eager to see Deirdre than she had ever thought possible. She drove to the store with a sense of joy, smiling as she parked the car in the lot. Her smile wavered a little as she passed the spot on the sidewalk where Umberto's body had been.

Deirdre, or someone, had evidently poured bleach on the concrete. Umberto was memorialized by a jagged white splotch containing scattered, faded bloodstains the shape of teardrops.

Let it go, Mariana thought.

She forced herself to smile again as she walked through the glass doors, smile as she greeted Alora.

"You only have two readings so far," Alora told her, holding out the card with the day's appointments. "And I hope you don't mind, but I need the room right at five, so I don't want to book anything for you after four thirty."

"What do you mean?" Mariana stopped short. She glanced at the card, noting that Alora had booked a half-hour at twelve thirty and another at two. Neither name was familiar. She returned the card to Alora. "What do you need the room for?"

"Deirdre said I could start doing readings." The young woman looked at her smugly.

"Oh. Congratulations, I guess. Where's Deirdre?"

"In Samantha's office."

"Do you have a silver chain I could hang this on?" A woman standing at the end of the counter waved a pendant with a deep blue stone of some kind in Alora's direction. "And what chakra does blue represent?"

"We have chains," Alora said, moving toward the customer, "right there in the case in front of you. And blue is the color of the third eye chakra."

"The throat chakra. The third eye is indigo." Mariana corrected Alora automatically. The girl turned back and glared, and Mariana realized that Alora had built up some resentment toward her. She hadn't been paying enough attention, and Alora was more than ready to steer appointments in her own direction.

Mariana started toward the back of the store, now with a second reason to talk to Deirdre.

She could hear the Reiki master's raised voice as she reached the hall. Deirdre and Samantha had left the door open, probably not having considered the possibility of a serious argument.

"You're making a mistake," Samantha was saying. "She doesn't have the training, and you know it."

"She'll learn," Deirdre replied calmly. "One learns by doing."

"One learns more by taking classes first," Samantha snapped.

Mariana froze in the doorway.

Samantha was standing behind her desk, braced on her arms, a pose that would have intimidated someone less self-possessed than Deirdre, especially considering the height difference. Samantha claimed to be five feet eleven. Mariana was certain the healer was actually a good six feet. Deirdre was maybe five foot five.

"I'm sorry—" Mariana began, but Samantha cut her off.

"This time I didn't mean you, although I'd be a lot happier with you if you had some formal training and picked up a couple of practitioner's certificates." Samantha's small office was crowded with shelves full of various herbal mixtures. But she had left enough wall space to show off her college degrees in pharmacy and nursing and her Reiki Master certification in both Usui and Karuna modes.

Samantha still looked like the nurse she had once been, dressing mostly in tailored blouses and skirts, favoring white, and wearing her grey hair cut close to her head. A flush of annoyance showed through the light makeup base that was her sole concession to vanity.

"I have a Reiki certificate," Mariana said. A master's degree in English didn't seem worth bringing up in this context.

"And that's a start," Samantha answered. "You have a basic education, you're a good listener, you genuinely care about the people who come to you, and you're an honest psychic. And I wasn't talking about you. Although I would feel better if you came to the Reiki workshops."

"Samantha is upset because I told Alora she could start booking her own readings," Deirdre said.

"Well—I wanted to say something about that, too," Mariana said. "I think there's a conflict of interest for her. I want her to book readings for me. Why would she do that if she could book them for herself—on the same day—instead?"

"I've told her that if a customer asks for you, she is not to mention that she is giving readings. And if a customer just asks generally about the availability of psychics, she should simply respond with who reads at what times," Deirdre replied.

"And you have confidence in her fairness?" Mariana asked.

"If you do, you're fooling yourself," Samantha said before Deirdre had a chance to answer. "That girl probably does have some psychic talent. Anybody who tries hard enough can develop some ability to read others. But she has no common sense, and no metaphysical background, and allowing her to call herself a psychic reader is not good for your store."

Jeff's door opened a little more than a crack. The hypnotherapist stuck his head into the hall. His dark hair was disheveled, his glasses slightly fogged, as if he might have been taking a nap.

"Could you please keep the noise down?" he asked. "I have a client here."

"I'm sorry," Mariana began.

"I'll take care of it," Deirdre said, then raised her voice to add, "Sorry, Jeff."

Jeff retreated and shut the door.

Samantha glowered.

"You've both made your points," Deirdre said. "And I'm still going to give her a chance. If problems arise, we'll deal with them. In the meantime, I have some jewelry to price."

Mariana moved into the office to allow Deirdre to leave.

"I do feel like the pot who called the kettle black," she said. She rested the bag containing her cards and her afternoon snack on Samantha's desk.

Samantha nodded. "A little humility is a good sign. But I've seen you wander through the book section when you aren't busy. You know you have a lot to learn, and you're willing to do the work. You're also smart enough that you don't get sidetracked by the crackpots."

"A pot but not a cracked one?" Mariana was pleased when Samantha smiled at that.

"I haven't yet heard you tell anyone about the alien space station off Santa Barbara," Samantha said. "Or predict the end of the world in our lifetime. You seem to be reading the Eastern mystics. I approve of that."

"I started searching for an explanation of why tarot works —why the right cards come up." Mariana found herself wanting more approval. "Even saying that the magic is in the reader, not in the cards, doesn't explain why a person concerned about love will draw Cups and one concerned about money will draw Pentacles. I can almost accept the concept of the specialized angels—the angels assigned to tarot duty who appear whenever a deck is shuffled—but not quite."

"Are you expecting to find something rational behind the magic?" Samantha asked.

"No, not rational." Mariana shook her head. "I've pretty much given up on rational since I've started working in the psychic realms. But so much associated with tarot has resonance with more generally accepted philosophies. The archetypes that Jung describes, forces of energy existing on the level of the collective unconscious, for one. The Magician, the High Priestess, the Empress, the Emperor, are all archetypes that Jung would recognize. The Kabbalah and the Tree of Life, for another, although I can sympathize with the scholars who insist that the only connection between the tarot and the Kabbalah is the significance attached to the number twenty-two."

"Good for you. I'm impressed," Samantha had stopped leaning on her desk about halfway through Mariana's riff on the tarot. She settled back into the tall chair behind it. "So how did you get from there to Eastern mysticism?"

"The Hindu mystic tradition, which seems to be the base of the Western metaphysical movement anyway, has never lost sight of the Goddess—the Divine Mother," Mariana replied. "I find that I can take some comfort in seeing myself as a descendant of the priestesses who acted as Her oracle. And yes, I know I just skipped from Asia to Old Europe."

"That's okay. You're making my point on the difference between encouraging you as a psychic reader, even with your lack of formal training in the field, and Alora as a psychic reader. Have you ever talked to her?"

"Not a lot." Mariana hadn't wanted to talk to Alora, but she didn't think she should say that.

"Because you knew it wouldn't be enlightening," Samantha said. "Try it sometime when you're certain you have control of your gag reflex. And don't laugh when she tells you we're all turning into crystals."

"Into crystals?"

Samantha nodded. "I haven't had the heart to inform her that getting stiff with age isn't the same thing as becoming a quartz."

Mariana laughed. "I don't think I want to hear more. And

there's something else I wanted to talk with Deirdre about."

"The murder on the doorstep?"

"Samantha, it was terrible. I'm not even certain why we're still going on as normal," Mariana said. "But I'm sure Deirdre told you everything all ready."

"She did. Of course it was a terrible experience for both of you, finding that man stabbed through the heart with a crystal." Samantha shook her head in sympathy. "And now Deirdre wants us all to come to the channeling this coming Saturday. Including Jeff. She's hoping Baba-ji will give us some information."

Mariana picked up her bag. "The experience was so terrible I can't look at the crystal, even though the detective offered to show it to me. And I don't want to come to the channeling. I guess I better talk to Deirdre."

"No appointments this afternoon?"

"Two, but I still have a little while before the first one."

"And you might want to spend some of it in the store, making certain Alora is booking a third for you."

"I know. I don't like snooping, but you're right. Thanks." Mariana was almost out the door, but then she turned to add, "I've thought about coming to the Reiki workshops. But I had a couple of experiences, placing hands on people, that were just too intense for me to handle. I believe it works. I just can't do it."

Samantha nodded. "Right now. You can't do it right now. Allow for growth, will you?"

"Of course. And thanks again."

Mariana left the small office and stopped at the reading room to leave her bag. Deirdre had said she would be pricing jewelry. That meant she was probably in the stock room, which doubled as her office.

In fact, Deirdre was sitting cross-legged on the floor, with little plastic bags of earrings spread out around her.

"Samantha says you want us all to come Saturday night," Mariana began.

"And you're going to tell me you don't want to do that," Deirdre finished.

"Well, yes."

"I can't force you, of course, but I would like to have you here. Something is wrong, and I think it may take all of us to set it right."

"I have come four times to your channelings, Deirdre, and two of the four have been followed by disasters. I know you're going to tell me that my coming to the channelings didn't cause disaster," Mariana hurried on before Deirdre could interrupt. "So I'll think about it. I was hoping some information had come to you in the last few days."

"Only that I'm supposed to channel on Saturday. Has anything come to you?"

"Not much. I went to Umberto's apartment on Monday. The detective was there, and he offered to let me go inside, but I couldn't do it."

"Because something is wrong." Deirdre hit the last word emphatically.

"If you know something is wrong, why are you making it worse with this Alora thing?" Mariana snapped.

"Sometimes it has to get worse before it gets better. Besides, I can't afford to lose her right now. I don't want to try to hire someone right after a murder on the doorstep. Don't you have a reading?"

"Yes. I do. One of only two that Alora has booked for this afternoon."

"Manifest more," Deirdre said calmly. "I have faith in you."

"Fine." Mariana said the word in a tone that was designed

to let Deirdre know that things weren't fine. When Deirdre ignored her, she decided not to pursue the matter.

Instead, she retreated to the reading room to set up her cards and get a cup of tea before her client arrived.

A woman in her mid-thirties, wearing a well tailored, silk-blend suit dyed a deep coral, was waiting just outside the room when Mariana returned with her tea. The suit, decorated with a silk scarf whose pattern featured the same deep coral, was so overwhelming that Mariana had trouble focusing on the woman's face. She was pale, with small features, dark eyes, and a lot of frizzy dark hair.

Mariana directed her to a chair and shut the door.

"Could you give me your name again?" Mariana asked. "I know it's on the card, but I'm afraid I don't remember."

The woman hesitated, then said, "Sally."

Mariana began to shuffle her cards. "Okay, Sally."

"You have your own cards." Sally seemed disappointed. "Of course you have your own cards."

"Yes?"

"I was hoping you would read these." Sally reached into a large black leather purse and pulled out a fat black velvet bag. She took a deck of cards out of the bag and handed them to Mariana.

The deck was one that Mariana had seen before, but not one that she liked. The imagery was explicitly sexual, the kind of sexuality that reminded her of orgies, not of love. Mariana sensed when she touched the deck that the designer had been playing with dark forces, attempting to misuse sexual energy to force his personal will on others. She was certain the designer was a man, although she had never bothered to check.

Of all the decks available, it was hard for her to understand why someone would choose this one. Nevertheless, she took the deck from the other woman's hands.

The deck was warm.

"You can read this deck," Mariana said. "You don't need me to read it."

"I do need you to read it. Would you mind?"

"It will be harder for me to be accurate if I use your deck. I chose one with images that I don't have to think about, images I find attractive. The pictures in this deck won't help—they'll distract. You can read this deck without me," she emphasized.

Sally put one hand on her forehead, as if trying to decide what to say.

"I have a split personality," she finally said. "It's my other self who can read the cards. I'm seeing a therapist, and she and I both thought that having these cards read might help me understand more about the other one, my other self. Will you help me? Please."

"Sure. If I can." Mariana took a deep breath and shuffled the cards. She shut her eyes and visualized the hawk on her shoulder. White light. She also needed to visualize the room filled with white light. Normally, she would ask the woman's guides to participate. This time she wasn't going to do that. She wanted the presence of the hawk firmly between her own energy and that of the woman's guides. She fanned the deck. "Pick ten."

Mariana laid out the cards and tried to decipher the unfamiliar pictures. The spread described a woman with worldly success who was weighed down with emotional problems. It also promised a spiritual transformation, whether Sally wanted one or not. Mariana passed on the information.

"Show me," Sally said.

Mariana went through the spread card by card, although that wasn't the way she normally read. Focusing on the meaning of individual cards cut off the flow of energy.

"Does that have resonance for you?" she asked.

Sally nodded. "I'm a real estate agent. That allows me to set my own hours, which sometimes I have to do. No one questions it if I'm not around for a day or two, as long as I call in. And yes, I make money."

"Are there questions you want to ask?"

"Do you think the Devil owns my soul?" Sally's voice was low, as if someone besides Mariana might be listening. But her face showed no emotion.

"No." Mariana snapped the word out. "I don't think the Devil owns anyone's soul. In fact, I don't believe in devils, except the ones we create."

"What do you believe in?"

"I believe all souls are moving toward the One, the Cosmic Spirit, that manifests as the Universe. I believe in the mystic tradition that underlies all major religions—but I reject the rituals. The Devil you talk about is simply a figure of speech, useful for the rituals of Christianity."

"I hope you're right," Sally said. She gathered up her cards and returned them to her bag.

"You still have some time," Mariana said. She had said too much, frightened the woman away, and she hadn't meant to do that. "If you don't have questions, I'll go with you to the counter and have Alora give you credit."

"No, thank you," Sally said. "You told me what I wanted to know."

Sally stood in the doorway for a moment, then nodded and left. Mariana struggled to find some sort of good-bye. But the woman was gone.

Mariana felt an urgent need for incense to clear the room. She didn't believe in the Devil, but she did believe in—she had experienced—the power that could be generated by the energy of a human being when it is channeled to inflict pain.

She forced herself to sit quietly, to breathe deeply. She didn't want to run into the woman at the front of the store.

And of course, the whole thing was silly. The woman's so-called other self was nothing but a nightmare caused by overwhelming emotional distress. Surely, the therapist would help her.

Mariana managed to avoid both Deirdre and Alora when she got the stick of incense. She was a little embarrassed by her reaction to the woman, and she didn't want to share it. Samantha's door was shut. So was Jeff's.

She stayed close to the reading room until her two o'clock client arrived.

This woman was closer to the normal client, if there was such a thing. She was wearing jeans and a loose sweatshirt, which did nothing to disguise the fact that she was fifty pounds overweight.

And she wanted to find out about her health.

When Mariana convinced her to discuss her health with Samantha, who could offer herbal mixtures to cleanse her liver and kidneys and dietary changes to counter the fat challenge, she asked about her love life.

All Mariana could see was a dark path.

"There's no one in your energy field at the moment," she said, automatically. She wondered how many times in the last few months she had said that. "But your path can change. And if you work on your health, you begin to shift the energy."

Tired. Mariana was tired. She dragged through the reading. And she wanted to go home.

She found herself grateful that Alora hadn't booked a late appointment.

She was on the white sand again, in the white tunic. The dragon-prowed ship was waiting for her, to take her into the mist.

This time she was carried to a verdant shore, ringed with low hills. The scene shifted to a country estate as she took two steps forward. During the voyage she had become a much younger girl, wearing a white dress with a long, full skirt.

A man in a brocade coat smiled as he saw her, and scooped her up in his arms, to dance with her.

Other men pulled them apart. She knew she was crying, even though she couldn't hear her own sobs. Someone hit her with the butt of a rifle. She shut her eyes. When she opened them again, she was in a dungeon, sitting on dirty straw.

And she knew that when the men came for her, she would be taken to the guillotine.

Not until after the blade came down was she permitted to leave the headless body, to float back to the dragon-prowed ship, to return to the mist.

Chapter Seven

On Friday morning, Mariana was still tired, groggy, almost as if she had a hangover. She had never felt this drained, not even after busy days at the store.

She thought about taking a walk, going to the park to visit Dorothy, but it was too much of an effort. Feeding the cats and getting ready to go took all the energy she had.

Friday afternoon was every bit as depressing as Thursday. This time Alora had only booked one reading for Mariana, an hour at three o'clock with a woman who had come to Mariana several times before. The woman kept hoping that something would change in her life, but not enough to change it herself. Mariana had learned that nothing she said would make any difference and that the way to fill the hour was simply to be still and let the woman talk. The psychic as storefront therapist.

Deirdre was behind the counter rearranging a display of necklaces when Alora handed Mariana the appointment card.

"That's all?" Mariana asked.

"That's all," Alora replied. "And I'll need the room at five again today."

"Oh." Mariana hoped that Deirdre would say something, but Deirdre ignored them. And Alora was waiting for a longer answer. Mariana considered a pitched battle, having it out, even quitting, but she was still feeling the effects of the almost sleepless night. She decided that this was not the moment. "Okay."

Alora smiled, and Mariana did her best to smile in return. She kept the forced grimace on her face until she reached Samantha's office.

"What am I going to do?" she asked, plopping herself in the chair next to Samantha's desk. She kept her voice low with effort.

"What are your choices?" Samantha answered. She had been weighing out herbs from several jars and mixing them into one of her concoctions. She stopped to listen.

"I can smile and watch that idiot child book readings for herself instead of for me. I can tell Deirdre she has to choose between us. I can quit." Mariana pulled her knees up and hugged herself. The room smelled of lavender and peppermint and something slightly medicinal and soothing.

"We're all a little tense right now," Samantha said, her voice as calm as if she had never had a tense moment in her life, "and none of those choices sound like something you ought to act on this afternoon. Another choice would include coming to class on Wednesday evenings, you know, to tune in to your abilities as a psychic healer. That might give you another perspective on Alora."

"I can't do that right now, I told you. I freeze when I even think about laying hands on another person. Too many strange things happened when I did that before." She had told Samantha about her psychic awakening when she had first come to Enchantment. The Reiki master had periodically attempted to convince Mariana to face her fears, and Mariana still resisted. "Working as an ordinary psychic is the best I can do, and that's almost beyond me. If I need a different perspective on Alora, it will have to come from another direction."

"Okay. I won't push it." Samantha said, but Mariana knew she only meant she was dropping it for the moment. "How about turning it over to your guides? Waiting until after the channeling tomorrow night to see what changes?"

"Don't remind me of the channeling. I don't want to come to the channeling. Another reason to quit." Mariana put her forehead on her knees and hugged tighter.

"Pretend you're your own client. What would you tell her?"

Mariana lifted her head. The combination of the herbal scent and Samantha's voice was calming her down. "I'd want to tell her to stop feeling sorry for herself, but I'd probably look for another way to phrase it. And I'd tell her not to act rashly. And I'd look for the brightest path of energy flow on a psychic level, but I can't do that for myself."

"Then I guess you'd better take care of your clients this afternoon and see if you can't come up with a bright energy path tomorrow." Samantha picked up one of the jars of herbs and put a spoonful on the scale.

"Thank you." Mariana stood and stretched out her spine. "Even though it is client, singular. Is there anything I can do for you?"

"Not today, but I'll remember that you offered."

Mariana left Samantha's office and moved down the hall to set up her table. Then she got herself a cup of tea and took *The Bhagavad Gita for Daily Living* from the shelves. It was going to be a long afternoon, and she figured she might as well learn something.

The reading with the sad woman went as she had expected. Mariana listened and nodded and barely said a word. She thought about leaving early, but ended up putting in her time, pretending to be a good sport, even if she didn't feel like one.

She got home in plenty of time to feed the cats and meditate, hoping to still her mind and shed the problems of the store—essentially switch gears in her psyche—and get ready to have dinner with Art. She was only partially successful.

Mariana heard the downstairs door open at a little after seven. Art was late, which wasn't his usual pattern. His feet thumped as he climbed the stairs.

She opened the door to her apartment when he was about halfway up.

He had cut his hair. The gray ponytail he had worn during their affair was gone. He had been able to tame most of the curl out of what remained, but one white strand had sprung loose to quiver on his forehead. His skin, which usually had the rich glow of coffee ice cream, lacked vitality.

Mariana hadn't dressed up for the evening. She was still wearing the long gauzy skirt and ruffled, white cotton blouse that she had worn to the store that afternoon.

Art was wearing a tan suit and white shirt. The only indication that he was no longer at work was the loose knot of his patterned tan and burgundy tie. He did something for the county, but Mariana couldn't remember what it was. She wondered if he had known Umberto. Probably not. It wasn't the same county. Art worked for L.A. County—not Ventura.

Looking at him, and having seen herself in the mirror moments before, she wondered how they had ever connected. She knew, though. For her, it had been the emotional equivalent of a wartime affair.

"I'm sorry," he began. "Freeway traffic."

"Not a problem. Hello."

"Hello."

"I just need to grab my purse." Mariana said it quickly, not wanting to ask him in.

Art paused on the stairs and nodded.

Getting her purse and keys and locking the door seemed to take a long, awkward time, made worse because Miles had heard Art's voice and tried to push past her to see him, but she convinced the cat to stay put, and then she was beside Art on the stairs, both of them smiling tensely.

"I made reservations," she said. "A neighborhood restaurant, not far. We can walk, if you like."

"Sure."

She walked down the stairs ahead of him, then waited just outside. Together, with enough space in between to acknowledge the tension, they walked to the corner and turned right on Thompson.

"How are things going at the store?" he asked.

"Not a subject for casual conversation," she answered. "I don't suppose the local murder made the L.A. papers."

"What?" Art stopped to look at her.

"I didn't know him," Mariana said. "He was found outside the store, that's all."

"I know you. That isn't all."

"Close enough. I'm getting along fine with Deirdre, and I have enough clients for readings that going over there is worthwhile." Close enough, she thought. That was close enough to the truth. She didn't want to revisit the situation with Alora.

"Are you sure you don't want to tell me about the murder?"

"There's really nothing to tell. A man I read for last Saturday afternoon was murdered that night, the police don't know who did it, and I can't pick anything up about it." She started walking again, and he fell into step beside her.

"That's a lot to tell. And I suspect there's more."

Mariana was silent.

"You're sure you're all right about it?" Art continued. "I told you, I have a sense you're in danger. How can you not be worried when someone was murdered practically at your front door?"

"I'm sure I'm all right. And I didn't know him, except for the reading, and I wasn't threatened. How are you?"

"Fine. Nothing new in my life." Art stopped again, this time grabbing her arm and pulling her in close.

Mariana stiffened and started to pull away, but then she realized he wasn't looking at her. He was looking at a group of five teenagers clustered on the corner ahead of them.

Three girls and two boys, dressed in black capes, their hair dyed deep black, their faces painted stark white with bright red lips, were evidently arguing over something.

"It's all right," Mariana said. "It's just the vampire children."

"What?"

"They're not really vampires," Mariana said. "But I think of them that way because of the Gothic excess of their costumes. As far as I know, they've never hurt anyone. And they draw so much attention to themselves by the way they dress that I'd be surprised if they start now."

"Gothic excess?"

"What would you call it?"

"Weird." Art was still staring at the teenagers, but he relaxed enough to let go of Mariana's arm.

"I haven't felt any sense of danger around them. Really." She resisted the impulse to rub the place where his fingers had been. He hadn't meant to hurt her, but he had.

Mariana turned again toward the corner, and Art followed. She nodded as they passed the small group.

The vampire children stopped talking to stare at her, eyes wide in mock horror.

For a moment she saw herself through their eyes, saw that she, too, could be seen as the weird one. When she heard the giggles behind her back, she realized that they had been indulging in their own little joke.

Art caught up with her as she was crossing the street.

"I didn't know Ventura was so exotic," he said.

"Ventura is one of those places where everyone I meet tells me how conservative Ventura is, but no one I meet is conservative," Mariana told him. "I think the conservatives and the artists somehow lead parallel lives that never touch."

Thompson Street was typical Small Town, U.S.A., though, so much so that she didn't need to point that out. A bowling alley, a paint and hardware store, a lube shop. A store that sold used clothing across from one that sold antiques and collectibles. Maybe the hooker motel—at least Mariana had heard it was a hooker motel—wasn't precisely true to the small town fantasy. But it was probably true to the reality.

Another block brought them to a cafe that served the Southern California version of soul food—baby lettuce salads, grilled vegetables, al dente pastas, fresh bread, great desserts. Fresh fish, not much meat.

Art nodded in recognition as they entered.

"You've been here before?" Mariana asked.

"No, but I know her cousins on both sides of the family," he answered. "There has to be a patio, but it's too cold to sit there tonight."

"You're right."

The dining area was crowded. Most of the tables were set close to the banquettes that lined three of the walls. Local art graced the space above the seats. More watercolors. Mariana loved the ubiquitousness of the local art. The fourth wall consisted of a large window that might have had a view of the ocean before the building across the street was built.

The people sitting at the tables, mostly in twos and fours, were dressed too modestly to be tourists, a sign of how late in the year it was. The restaurant, while more than a mile from the beach, attracted a T-shirts-and-shorts crowd from May to September. Even so, Art was the only man in a suit.

A cheerful Hispanic youth in a white shirt and slacks trotted toward them from the bar area, an even smaller room to their right.

"I hope you have reservations," he said.

Mariana assured him that they did.

The youth escorted them to a table next to the patio door. Mariana took the banquette side, and Art sat across from her.

Ordering was easy. She wanted the pasta with mushrooms, he wanted the fresh grilled sea bass, they both wanted salads and white wine.

When the young man had left, Mariana waited for Art to say something. She was hoping for a casual topic, not something with fear or urgency. If she could think of a casual topic, she'd raise it herself.

He studied her face for a moment before he began. "Sometimes I think I'm being haunted," he said.

"By what?" she asked. "Or whom?"

"I don't know. I wake up in the night thinking someone is there, but I'm alone." As he said the words, Mariana could see the fear in his eyes.

"Art, that's a sleep disturbance. It doesn't mean you're being haunted. Sleep disturbances come from anxiety about any number of things. Including the fact that you really were attacked once from the astral plane." She felt silly saying that, but it was true. "It's a lot more likely that you're having some kind of dream flashback than it is that it's happening again."

"I thought you'd take me seriously," he said.

"I do take you seriously." Again, that was close enough to the truth. She would take him more seriously if he didn't sound pouty.

"But that's the kind of rational response I would have expected from someone else, not from you," he said.

"I know. Especially since so much of my life is taken up by the non-rational. But tonight, at least, I'm not sensing any strange energies around you. Just a lot of unhappiness." Mariana didn't want to go on. If he was unhappy because of her, there was nothing she was willing to do about it.

"Will you tell me if you think there is something going on around me?"

"Of course." She sighed inwardly. She would ask the hawk later, when she was alone, but she really wasn't sensing a problem. What she was sensing was that he wanted an excuse to see her. And the fear in his eyes was fear of rejection. Under the circumstances, that fear wasn't irrational.

Finding another topic of conversation wasn't easy. They drifted through dinner, with long periods of silence. Even though the food was good, Mariana had trouble enjoying it.

Art used to be cheerful and unflappable and good company. That was the Art she had almost fallen in love with. This Art was moody. Mariana didn't want to be around moody if she didn't have to—if she wasn't paid to—which was part of the toll working at Enchantment was taking on her.

When the waiter offered them coffee and dessert, she shook her head.

"I have to work tomorrow," she said, more to Art than the waiter, letting him know that she wanted to leave.

"Not even another glass of wine?"

"Especially not wine. I barely drink at all anymore. Even a second glass would give me a headache. I suspect it has something to do with working from open chakras in my head."

"Are you sure what you're doing is worth it?"

"No. I just don't know what else to do." That was more honesty than she had intended. But she couldn't take it back.

They were in the street again and headed back to her place when she decided to ask him after all.

"Did you ever happen to run across someone named Umberto—or Bert—Marconi? Working for the county?"

Art didn't answer right away.

"I don't think so," he finally said, "but I've been there a long time, and I might have forgotten. Why?"

"He's the person who was murdered, whose body was left outside Enchantment. And he might have worked for Ventura County in some way. L.A. County, Ventura County. I knew it was a long shot, but I thought I'd ask," Mariana replied.

"Now will you tell me how you're involved?"

"I don't know that I am. I had read for him that afternoon, and the body was left at Enchantment's door. The detective thought it might be some kind of macabre message for me. But I haven't been able to pick anything up more about him and neither has Deirdre."

They passed the corner where the vampire children had been standing. The five teenagers were gone.

"Mariana, if you can't pick anything up, that means you may be involved somehow, you know that. Deirdre too. What are you going to do next?"

"Go to Deirdre's channeling tomorrow night. Her request."

"Do you mind if I come, too?"

Mariana wanted to tell him that she did mind, but the words didn't come out. She found herself giving directions to Enchantment instead.

94

"Why can't I just pick you up at your place?" Art asked. "We could go together."

"No. I won't have a lot of time between my afternoon appointments and the evening channeling, and I don't want to have to coordinate with anyone." That felt good. She had needed to assert herself, even if only a little.

Art didn't respond. Sulking again, Mariana thought. They walked in silence until they reached the door to her building.

"I'm not asking you up," she said.

"That's okay. I'll see you tomorrow."

Mariana held out her hand. "Thank you for dinner. I don't get out often, and I enjoyed it."

"And thank you." There was a trace of amusement in his voice, the old Art, as he picked up her overdone courtesy. "Goodnight."

He clicked his heels and bowed.

"Goodnight."

She let herself in and trudged up the stairs, as tired as she had been the night before.

This time, though, she slept.

When she left the dragon-prowed ship, she was wearing a loose home-spun skirt and a full blouse with a tight bodice. She started running in her bare feet as she reached the grass, running for the dirt road, knowing he would meet her there.

He came in a horse-drawn buckboard, waving when he saw her smiling, laughing as he pulled her up onto the seat beside him, bright eyes shining.

The children were waiting at the farmhouse.

She was granted many years of joy before he died, and then years of joy with another man with bright eyes before she was called back to the dragon-prowed ship, back to the land on the other side of time.

Who . . .

Chapter Eight

There would be a full circle for the Saturday night channeling. Mariana knew that when she woke in the morning. Everyone who needed to be present for whatever was supposed to happen would be in the proper seat. Something about the sunlight streaming through the slits in the mini-blinds was reassuring, and for that moment she put aside any reservations about the evening ahead.

Miles was fast asleep, curled against her throat and chest, partly under the covers. She moved him just enough so that she could slip out of bed.

Ella was waiting for her in the meditation chair.

Mariana lifted the Siamese up so that she could sit, then resettled the cat on her lap. The purring cat and the uninterrupted meditation confirmed her sense of peace. She felt rested, rested enough to walk—not drive—to the Farmers Market, where she could select food for the coming week with a sense of joy.

She even had time to walk by way of Cemetery Park.

It was midmorning, and the sun was pleasantly warm, when Mariana left the apartment and turned north toward the former graveyard. The longer than usual trip would eat up all the time available, so she set herself a swift pace.

Hello!

The word reached her as she placed her foot on

the first stone step.

Hello, Dorothy, Mariana thought in reply.

She nodded to the other copper plaques as she ascended the grassy slope to the tree that shaded the graves of Dorothy and her parents.

Dorothy offered a little flurry of energy as Mariana sat cross-legged on the grass. Mariana recognized it as a hug.

I'm glad to see you, too, she thought, even as she realized that she didn't exactly see Dorothy—she just sensed her presence.

Mariana wasn't the only human in the park. Another woman sat cross-legged on a blanket several yards down the slope and to Mariana's right as she looked toward the ocean. The woman appeared to be meditating in silence. Mariana accepted her as a kindred spirit and closed her own eyes.

Peace. She held the moment, then opened her eyes again. Her eyes landed on Thomas's marker, Dorothy's father. For the first time she noticed that he was Thomas Spiers Sr. That meant there was a Thomas Spiers Jr. Dorothy had a brother.

Mariana sent Dorothy a query about her brother.

Dorothy didn't have an answer. She didn't seem to remember her brother, just as she didn't remember the baby who had cost her her life.

"I remember my brother." Mariana said it out loud, then felt a little embarrassed. "My brother saw the woman in the corner of the room, too."

Dorothy sent a polite question mark about the woman, but Mariana knew she wasn't really interested. Dorothy was only interested in her own static energy, though she seemed to like it that Mariana could communicate with her.

Mariana answered anyway, really for herself. When she and Brian had been about three years old, Mariana had seen an old woman in a blue cape in the corner of their bedroom.

Mariana screamed, and Linda came running in to see what the matter was. Linda was mad, of course, Linda was always angry at her children in those days before she became sad and nervous, so Brian didn't say that he had seen the woman, too.

Years later he told her, when he said he was going to look for a spiritual teacher. But that evening was a memory for another time. If she thought about it now, she would only make herself late. Now it was time to leave the park for the market and then get ready for work.

Good-bye, Dorothy, Mariana thought.

Good-bye.

Mariana hurried on along Main. The small stores, many converted houses, gave way to a more formal downtown dominated by a new movie multiplex and chain restaurants. The older buildings, the thrift stores and collectible shops were more inviting, but the franchises paid more rent.

She glanced up California Street, up the spacious steps to the City Hall, and stopped a moment to take in the statue of Father Junipero Serra. A monument to a man who had destroyed a way of life, a community, in the name of progress, though he called it Christianity. That time the change was tragedy, this time farce.

At the next block she turned left to the Farmers Market, breathing deeply. She stopped at the stall run by the chunky man in the Dodgers cap and picked up some dark green spinach, imagining a creamy soup. Carrots, potatoes, onions. Fruit, too, heavy pink grapefruit, and more greens for salad. A lot to carry. But worth it.

"Looks like you're having company," the man said.

Mariana shook her head. "No. Just taking care of myself."

By the time she got back to her apartment, Mariana's energy was bubbling through her body. The brief contact with Dorothy reminded her that someone could be simply happy in her presence, even if that someone was a spirit that refused to leave her own grave. And the kind man at the Farmers Market had completed the refreshment of her spirit.

She put the greens in the refrigerator, stacked the grapefruit in a bowl, and quickly threw together a sandwich on some honey wheat bread from the bakery on Thompson. By the time she was ready to leave, she felt prepared to face the business of the store.

The afternoon turned out to be a profitable one, at last, with five clients, and Alora too busy to waylay any of them. All five were women, and all five were looking for fairy tale princes to transform their lives, and only one of the five had a man anywhere around her energy field.

As usual, Mariana didn't like disappointing the other four —she wondered if she would ever be able to disappoint clients without caring—but three of them easily accepted her reading, so easily that she knew none of them expected rescue anyway.

The fourth was an overweight woman with a sad, round face, Luisa.

"There's a curse on me, isn't there?" she asked.

"No, there's no curse. There just isn't a man," Mariana replied.

"But that's because of the curse," Luisa insisted. "Everyone has a soul mate. I read the love poetry, I know there is a true Beloved. I can't find mine because of the curse."

"The true Beloved in sacred love poetry refers to the Higher Self. It's like falling in love with your own soul. Your true soul mate is yourself," Mariana said.

"No. My true soul mate is a man, and he is somewhere, but I cannot find him," Luisa said. "Another psychic told me that. She said the curse is why I'm so unhappy all the time, and nothing ever works out for me. She told me that she would pray for the curse to be removed. I thought you might do that, too."

"Luisa, if you want to be happy, then you have to do something to make yourself happy. That won't come from someone else praying," Mariana said. "If you want your future to be different, then you have to act differently."

Luisa just stared, and Mariana knew that arguing was useless.

She was glad to see Luisa leave, especially since then it was time to go home and feed the cats.

Mariana delayed at home as long as she could before coming back to the store. She didn't feel like chatting with anyone who might be coming to the channeling, with the possible exception of Samantha, and she had already claimed enough of the Reiki master's time and support.

When Mariana finally entered the classroom, the circle was set. Deirdre was in her usual chair, but somehow Samantha had ended up next to her, where Lena liked to sit. Lena sat glowering on Deirdre's left, arms crossed in annoyance.

Stella and Bernard had split up, Bernard next to Samantha, Stella next to Lena.

Alora was sitting next to Stella.

"Tonight will certainly be exciting, won't it?" Stella was saying, to no one in particular. "And to think we missed it all last week! Well, not really all of it, of course, but the police. We missed the police."

Mariana considered pointing out that seeing Umberto's body hadn't exactly been a blessing, but instead just tuned her out.

Art sat in the center of one of the three remaining chairs, an empty one on each side. When he saw Mariana, the gloom left his face and he smiled, almost his old open smile. Tonight he had dressed down, jeans and an open-necked Oxford cloth shirt, but he still looked out of place with the others. Too normal somehow.

Something was wrong with the symmetry, the chairs weren't placed quite right. But Deirdre must have done that intentionally, Mariana thought. She started toward the chair that would put her between Art and Bernard, but Jeff pushed past her.

"Sorry I'm late," he said, taking the chair.

His hair was rumpled and his cotton shirt was wrinkled. Mariana tried to remember if she had ever seen Jeff when he didn't look as if he had just been rudely awakened from a nap. An instance didn't spring to mind.

"I'm late, too," Mariana said, reluctantly slipping into the vacant one between Art and Alora.

"We're starting right on time," Deirdre said. "The universe unfolds at the proper moment."

"It always does," Stella said, smiling and nodding.

No one else felt compelled to comment on Deirdre's wisdom.

"Is there anything anyone needs before we start?" Deirdre asked. When no one spoke up, she continued. "Then find a comfortable position, and focus for a moment on your breath. I want to have us better aligned before I begin the channeling."

Mariana shut her eyes and followed the course of her breath.

"Breathe in, breathe out," Deirdre said. "Breathe down to your toes, and let the breath carry away your tension."

Within a few breaths, Mariana could feel herself relaxing. More than that, she could feel both Art and Alora relaxing. She almost didn't mind sitting next to Alora now that she was relaxed.

Something wasn't quite right, though, someone wasn't relaxed. She heard that someone get up and move toward the door connecting the classroom to the alley.

She opened her eyes and saw that Samantha's chair was empty.

Samantha was quietly ushering Detective Claybourne into the room. She shook her head at Mariana, letting her know that she didn't have to get up.

The chairs had been arranged with enough space so that Samantha could add one without disturbing anyone but herself. That was why they hadn't seemed quite right earlier.

The detective joined the group. He caught Mariana's eyes and mouthed "Hello."

The disturbance was enough, though. Eyes flew open around the circle.

"I believe that all of you have met Detective Claybourne at some point during this past week," Deirdre said. "Those who wish to talk with him may do so after the channeling. Please close your eyes again and focus on your breath."

Everyone did as told.

Mariana allowed the thought that Claybourne's presence was the reason Deirdre had asked everyone to come to the channeling to pass through her mind without comment. The wish that Deirdre had let her know Claybourne was coming passed through her mind without comment as well. And then she forced her attention back to her breath.

Deirdre waited until the breaths were more or less quiet and synchronized, and then led them through a rainbow meditation, to raise the vibration of their chakras. She ended by saying, "If you wish, you may open your eyes. Remain seated comfortably in your chairs while I summon Baba-ji."

The overhead lights in the room had been turned off. The only illumination came from four white candles on a low table in the center of the circle. But the dimness made it easier for

Mariana to see the glow of Deirdre's aura as she shut her eyes and allowed Baba-ji to come through.

"Good evening, dear ones." The voice was still Deirdre's, but stronger, more self-possessed. "I welcome you all, especially the newcomers. As we spend this time together, I encourage you to release the emotional turmoil that brought you here, even if not all of your questions are answered in the manner you are hoping for. I will give the information that it is appropriate for you to receive, and no more. This evening I will begin to my right."

"I have no questions, Baba-ji," Samantha said.

"No, you would not," the voice replied. "You have many skills in this lifetime, and one of them is the ability to find the answers that you need without directly asking the spirit world for guidance. The guidance is a part of you, and you are the stronger for that."

Samantha turned to Detective Claybourne, who was next in line. "Ask," she said quietly.

"Baba-ji, I am here in search of information about the violence that occurred in front of this store a week ago." The detective's face became flushed as he spoke. "What can you tell me?"

Deirdre was quiet for a long time. Finally, the voice said, "I can tell you that you will find the person you seek. I can also tell you that the entity who discarded his body that night is not interested in revenge. On the human level, his life was taken because of a mistaken belief system. This cycle is not yet ended. The challenge is one that you are prepared for, however. And on the karmic level, all will be in balance."

"I'm glad my arrest record gets a gold star," Claybourne said. "Any suggestions on where I should look for this person?"

"This person is near. You may stumble over this person if

you are not careful. That is all that you are to know this evening." Deirdre shifted restlessly in the chair, then settled down. "Does the next person have a question?"

"No question, Baba-ji," Bernard said.

The voice said nice things to Bernard and then to Jeff, who didn't have any questions, either.

"I don't quite know how to ask this, Baba-ji," Art began. "I feel haunted. Or hunted. What is going on?"

"You are haunted by your own feelings, dear one, and hunted by your own need to rise to a higher level. You are also sensitive to the challenges that a loved one must face, though the challenges are not your own, and this is causing you some distress. Again, remember that all is and will be in balance, and seek peace within, whatever appears to be happening without." Deirdre shifted again in her chair.

Mariana wondered what was going on that made Deirdre so restless. She was usually still throughout the channeling.

"No questions, Baba-ji," Mariana said.

"Very good, dear one," the voice replied.

"I have a question Baba-ji," Alora said.

"Yes, dear one," the voice said.

Mariana resisted annoyance. She had hoped for a few more kind words from Baba-ji, and now she wouldn't get them. Her own fault. She could have asked a question.

"When will I be able to make a living as a psychic?" Alora asked.

"Although this is not the answer you wish to hear, dear one, it is the one you must be given," the voice replied. "Your destiny in your current incarnation does not include the opportunity to be of service in the manner you describe. Your path lies in another direction. It is to be hoped that you will embrace this path and know that all is for the best."

Alora grimaced. "I have no more questions, Baba-ji."

Mariana couldn't help feeling relieved. Maybe Deirdre had been right after all, to give Alora an opportunity and then insist she come to the channeling to hear the truth. Maybe things would be better.

"I just want to hear whatever you have to tell me," Stella said. "Although my son is still seeing that girl, and I still think there's something wrong with her, so anything you can do to help would be appreciated."

"You must allow your son to create and fulfill his own destiny, dear one," the voice said.

Mariana closed her eyes. She paid enough attention to the rest of the channeling to confirm that none of it had anything to do with the store generally or Umberto's murder specifically.

Baba-ji assured Stella and Lena that they were on their spiritual paths, as always, and then Deirdre took over her own vocal chords again.

"Would anyone like to share an experience with the group?" she asked. When no one volunteered, she turned to Claybourne. "What can we do for you?"

"I was hoping for some useful information," he replied. "Either from the channeling itself or from someone who was here last week. I thought maybe coming back here—"

"To the scene of the crime," Stella whispered.

Claybourne's mouth twitched. "In a manner of speaking, yes. I thought coming back this week might remind one of you of something you saw or heard that was out of the ordinary."

"I've been thinking about it all week," Stella said. "I just wish we could help."

Bernard nodded. Lena still looked unhappy. Nothing that Baba-ji had said made up for not getting the chair she thought of as her own.

106

"All right, then." Claybourne stood. "You all know how to get in touch with me."

That became the signal for everyone to stand.

Samantha turned on the lights.

Mariana shut her eyes briefly. The brightness was always a shock.

"See you Monday," Jeff said, already halfway toward the door to the hall.

"See you Monday," Samantha echoed. She glanced at the others and started after him. "I just need to close my office and I'll be out of here."

"I guess there's nothing we can do," Stella said.

"No." Bernard tugged at her arm. "We might as well go home. Lena, we'll walk you to your car."

"Goodnight." Stella looked around as if hoping someone would stop them. When no one did, she allowed Bernard to escort her out the door to the alley, Lena following.

Deirdre started to lock the door behind them, then paused and looked at Art.

Art picked up Mariana's hand. She squeezed his for an instant and then pulled away.

"Can I talk you into coffee or a drink?" he asked.

"Not tonight."

"Baba-ji meant you, you know. I'm picking up someone else's danger, and it's yours." He moved a step toward the door, then took the same step back.

"Maybe. I'll be fine. Really." Mariana didn't want to have this discussion in front of Claybourne. "Goodnight, Art. We'll talk soon. I promise."

"Okay. Please be careful. Goodnight." Art walked slowly toward the door.

Deirdre held it open for him, then locked it behind him.

"We can leave through the store," she said.

"Before we leave, I'd like to know what was different tonight. What did you notice?" Claybourne asked.

"More people," Mariana said. "And Deirdre was restless."

"I kept feeling as if another entity was trying to get through," Deirdre said. "At the same time that Baba-ji was there, something else wanted in."

"I don't suppose you'd like to let it in tonight," Claybourne said.

"No." Deirdre said it firmly, then laughed. "No, I don't want to do that. But if I pick up anything, I will of course let you know."

Deirdre and Mariana each picked up two of the candles, blew them out, and replaced them on the table.

"We can leave the chairs," Deirdre said.

Mariana picked up her bag and started down the hall, Claybourne behind. Jeff's door was closed, no light showing. Samantha had left her door open, but the office was dark.

"Are you sure you don't want food or drink?" Claybourne asked.

"I'm sure. But thank you for asking," Mariana said. He looked disappointed, so she added, "Maybe another time."

They waited by the front door while Deirdre turned off the lights and set the burglar alarm.

On the sidewalk beyond the parking lot, Mariana could see two black-caped figures hurrying along. Vampire children, she thought. She wondered what vampire children did on Saturday night.

"Did you see where Alora went?" Deirdre asked.

"No, why?" Mariana answered.

"Because her car is there." Deirdre unset the burglar alarm and turned the lights back on. "I don't want to shut her in. Wait here."

Mariana and Claybourne waited while Deirdre walked back through the store. They could hear her check the restroom, check the offices.

"Alora?" she called.

"I'll check her car," Claybourne said. "Which one is it?"

"It's the black Honda." Mariana pointed to the car.

Claybourne pushed through the door and jogged the short distance to the Honda. Mariana watched as he peered first into the front seat, then the back. He stood for a moment with his hands on his hips, looking around to see if there were somewhere Alora could reasonably be found. The other stores in the strip mall—the discount hair salon, the dry cleaner, and the video rental shop—were closed, lit only by dim night lights. Claybourne walked slowly back to Mariana.

Deirdre had also returned without the young woman.

"Is there anywhere around here she might have walked to?" Claybourne asked.

"No," Mariana said. "There's nothing around here open at night."

The three of them looked at one another.

"Has something happened to her?" Claybourne asked.

"I think so," Mariana whispered.

"Yes," Deirdre said. "Alora's gone."

The air was dry and dusty. The sand wasn't the sand of the beach. It was brown and thin beneath her bare feet.

The wind was blowing, and she had trouble standing.

There was something she was supposed to see, but she couldn't see it.

What am I supposed to see, she cried into the wind.

But the wind blew the words back in her face.

Chapter Nine

"What do you mean, gone?" Claybourne asked.

"I mean she isn't nearby, that's all," Deirdre said. "I didn't mean she's dead, or anything like that."

The three of them stood by the front door. Deirdre had deposited her carryall on the counter above the jewelry case, demonstrating that she was no longer in a hurry to leave.

Mariana continued to look out at the dimly lit parking lot.

"The vampire children," she said. "I saw two vampire children, but one of them could have been Alora."

"And what do *you* mean?" Claybourne asked. His mouth was set in a way that made Mariana wonder if he was rethinking his willingness to work with psychics.

"The teenagers who wander around downtown Ventura in black capes and white makeup," she said. "You must have seen them."

"Alora doesn't hang out with them," Deirdre said. "She's a bit older, and she thinks they're silly."

It was a measure of how concerned Mariana was that she didn't comment on what Alora might find silly.

"You mean you saw two figures in black capes," Claybourne said, glaring at Mariana. "You don't mean you saw vampires."

"Well, yes."

"Where were they?"

"Across the street. Walking toward the mountains." Both Claybourne and Deirdre stared at her, so Mariana added, "I know the mountains are miles from here. I have trouble with directions. I tend to frame everything as toward the mountains or toward the ocean."

"Is it like Alora to walk away without saying good-bye? Leaving her car?" Claybourne asked.

Deirdre shook her head.

"She was disappointed in what Baba-ji told her, though," Mariana said. "Maybe she left in a huff."

"No," Deirdre said. "I don't believe it."

"We could both still be spooked about what happened last week," Mariana said. "That would affect our ability to sense what's going on."

"I still don't believe it," Deirdre said.

"All right," Claybourne said, holding his hands up in a gesture of surrender. "Why don't you give me Alora's address? I'll ride around a little tonight, look for the two caped figures, come back and see if Alora's car is still here, and then check to see if she found another way home. I think that's all we can do until tomorrow."

"He's right," Mariana said.

"I'll have to get her address from the file." Deirdre walked toward the back of the store for the second time.

"I want to ride with you," Mariana said.

"You don't have to. But I do want to make certain that you get home safely," Claybourne replied.

"I would feel better if I rode with you. I need to see where she lives for myself."

"Okay. But if I ask you to stay in the car, will you do that?"

Mariana didn't want to promise anything. She managed a nod.

Deirdre returned with Alora's address on a slip of paper,

and handed it to Claybourne.

"I know it's off Sanjon, near the railroad tracks," she said.

"Thanks. Do you want me to follow you home?" Claybourne asked.

"No. I'll be fine. Look for Alora."

The three of them left the store. Mariana carefully stepped past the place where Umberto's body had been the week before. Claybourne and Mariana watched as Deirdre set the alarm, walked to her car, and drove away.

"Deirdre really is fine," Mariana said. "Or as fine as any of us can be under the circumstances."

Claybourne led her to his car, a light blue Saturn. Once they were inside and settled, he said, "Tell me about Alora."

"I wish you had asked Deirdre. Deirdre knows her better than I do."

"But you've worked around her enough to draw a few conclusions, even if you haven't picked up anything psychic." As he talked, he started the car and pulled out of the parking space. He turned right coming out of the parking lot, heading in the general direction of the mountains. The neighborhood quickly changed, the dimly lit small stores and brightly lit asphalt parking of the mini-mall giving way to dimly lit small houses and dark sidewalks.

"Yes. I'm afraid that my conclusions aren't very helpful, though. They're closer to judgments."

"You don't like her, that's clear. So start with that. Tell me why not."

"Oh, dear." Mariana sighed. "No, I don't like her. I find her arrogant and ignorant, and every time I think that, I think how arrogant and ignorant I am to judge her and find her lacking."

"Then tell me about her behavior, not her character. I don't want you to feel bad." He glanced at her, clearly amused, then turned back to the street, driving slowly so that they could check both sides, looking for some kind of movement in the shadows. "Would it be like her to run off, just to worry everybody? Just to gain attention?"

"I don't think so. I think if she wanted attention, she would be more likely to cause an emotional scene in front of everyone. Disappearing quietly doesn't feel right, not for Alora."

Claybourne drove the next few blocks in silence.

"Well, your vampire children seem to have disappeared," he said, making a slow U-turn. "Let's see if Alora has gone back to her car."

They drove back to the store in silence, to find the Honda still sitting in the parking lot.

"Are you sure you want to ride with me to her place?" Claybourne asked.

"I'm sure. I don't think she's there, but I'd like to know."

The address Deirdre had given them was not far from where Mariana lived. But it was only when they were almost there that Mariana realized it would have made sense to bring her own car so that Claybourne didn't have to drive her back to the store. She felt comfortable riding with him, and she had wanted to hold onto the feeling a little while longer.

The apartment building was three stories of stucco that had once been white, but was now cracked and peeling to the point where gray dominated. There were no lights showing.

"Stay in the car," Claybourne said. "I'll be right back."

Mariana would have argued, but she knew he was right. Alora wasn't going to be found. And while she didn't sense danger, she also didn't think anything would be gained by wandering around in the night.

Claybourne strode along a walk made of badly cracked cement to what had once been a security door. Mariana watched him enter and disappear into a dark hall.

The narrow street was deserted. Trees cast shadows from a half moon, with no light to chase them away. The faint chug of a freight train, running along an embankment only a few yards away, grew until the roar shook the car, then subsided. Trees blocked the sight, but not the sound, of the track and the freeway just beyond. This was not a place anyone would live by choice, and Mariana felt an unexpected pang of pity for Alora.

Claybourne emerged from the darkness, shaking his head.

"I didn't pound on the door," he said as he got into the car. "But I knocked loudly enough that she would have heard me. And then that train came by, loud enough to wake the dead. Any other ideas?"

"No. Not tonight."

"I'll come back here in the morning. And I'll let you know if I find anything. You might oblige me by staying home tomorrow, or at least staying out of this area."

"I might," Mariana replied. "On the other hand, I often take walks around the neighborhood, and I don't live far from here. Besides, if something has happened to Alora, it happened at the store, not here. I don't think anything is happening here."

"We don't know yet that anything has happened to Alora anywhere. Maybe a friend picked her up." Claybourne pulled away from the curb and headed back toward the store.

"And we wouldn't even be particularly worried if Umberto hadn't been murdered on our doorstep a week ago."

"But he was." Claybourne slowed down and glanced at Mariana. "I'm off duty, and I could use a glass of something to unwind."

"Won't your wife object? I'm not saying that from anything psychic," she added quickly. "You're wearing a ring."

"My wife has been married to a cop for a lot of years," he said. "She accepts a lot of things without question, if not always happily. One of them is that I occasionally have a drink after work. Besides, I may get you to say something over a glass of wine that will give me a clue about what direction to pursue."

"I thought you were off duty."

"My head is always on."

"Okay. On one condition, though. You have to tell me your first name." Claybourne smiled, so Mariana added quickly, "Please don't ask me to guess. I'm a psychic, but not a mind reader. There's a difference."

"My first name is David. I would have told you before, if I'd thought of it. And I'd like to know the difference, but you can tell me over that drink."

"David. That's a heavyweight biblical name," Mariana said.

"I think my mother thought of it more as a heavyweight family name—I share it with my grandfather."

"That isn't what I thought your name would be," Mariana said, puzzled that the name didn't seem right. She started to follow a stray thought, then shook her head to come back to the moment. "I'll tell you what I can about my psychic abilities. Briefly, I'm an empath, not a telepath. I can pick up what people are feeling, but not what they are thinking."

"I'm not certain I understand the difference."

"I didn't either, before I started doing this. I think the first time I heard the word empath was on *Star Trek*." She was pleased that he smiled at the reference. "I also ought to warn you that I can't drink very much anymore—I lost my tolerance when I started reading, I'm not certain why—but I could handle one glass."

"One glass is fine. That's all I have time for."

116

Claybourne had been driving slowly east on Thompson. He pulled the car over to the curb. Mariana realized that they were across the street from the same small restaurant and bar where she had eaten the night before with Art.

"Is this all right?" Claybourne asked.

"This is fine."

"Do you want to get your car first?"

"I thought about that. But I think I'd rather check on Alora's car after we've given her a little more time to get back to it."

Claybourne turned off the engine. "I thought you might."

"See, you're psychic, too," Mariana said.

"My wife would disagree." He smiled, but the words were dry.

Mariana opened the car door and stepped out. She walked around to join him, then resisted the impulse to take his arm as they crossed the street.

The same young Hispanic in the white shirt opened the door for them. He nodded, recognizing Mariana from the night before.

"Welcome back," he said.

"Thank you." She felt herself blushing.

"I'm afraid we don't have a table," the young man said to Claybourne.

"Room at the bar?"

The young man nodded and stepped out of their way.

Claybourne placed his hand on Mariana's back, guiding her toward the small room with the bar.

The bartender, a blonde woman wearing an apron over a man's white shirt and jeans, was listening intently to the only other patrons, a couple at the far end. She glanced over as Claybourne and Mariana sat and excused herself to wait on them.

"White wine," Mariana said.

"Make it two."

"I can give you the house white, or we have a pretty good Chardonnay on special tonight, for just a little more."

"The Chardonnay," Claybourne said.

The bartender nodded. In one smooth move, she picked up two glasses in her left hand, a bottle with her right, filled the glasses, and deposited them on napkins.

Claybourne had his wallet out and a twenty on the bar before Mariana could stop him.

"Next time is on you," he said. "I gather you come here often."

"Not really. It's just that I was here last night."

"With the African American man who came to the channeling session hoping you would leave with him, the one who worries about you?"

"Yes. But there's nothing between us. Really."

"I didn't mean to pry." He paused while the bartender delivered his change. When she had returned to her conversation, he added, "Now tell me more about your psychic power."

"I don't think of it as power," Mariana answered. "I have a talent that allows me to tune in to the energy around people, I often pick up their feelings as well, and I have a spirit guide that sometimes brings me information. But it's limited. I can't always get the information I ask for. And when my ego gets in the way, as it does when I have a stake in the situation, I sometimes think I'm getting guided information when I'm really just tuning in to my own hopes and fears. So I'm wrong."

"Why do you have a spirit guide and other people don't?"

"Everybody has guides," Mariana took a sip of her wine. "This is good. Thank you."

"You're welcome. But if everyone has guides, everyone should be psychic."

"Well, everyone is, of course. Or could be. No matter what your wife says." Mariana said it without thinking, then wished she hadn't, and hurried on. "Most people don't try to tune in to the energy flow around them. Or when they do get information, they call it hunches, gut feelings. They don't identify the source. People who say they don't have guides will sometimes admit to guardian angels, or dream messages from a dead grandmother. Sometimes it's just a question of vocabulary."

"Can you tell anything about my guides?"

"Not under these circumstances. Please, no tests. Tests make me nervous. Umberto had to test me when I read for him."

Claybourne frowned. "You told me something about his guide. Who was it again?"

"White Eagle. I can't always get a name, but White Eagle is famous, so when I got the image of all the white feathers, I took a shot, and I was right."

"How is White Eagle famous?"

"There's a bunch of books, channeled information, about White Eagle. I wish I could tell you I've read them, but I haven't."

"Would it help me to read the books?" Claybourne asked.

"I don't think so," Mariana replied, shaking her head. "You can try them if you want, but they were written a long time ago by a channel who comes across as naïve today. Besides, spirit guides aren't bound by space and time. Some, especially the high ones, will act as guides for more than one person at a time. Baba-ji is one of those. Deirdre channels him, but so do a lot of other people. And because people are fallible and connections imperfect, a spirit can sound different, depending on the human involved."

"I'll take your word for it. Can you tune in to White Eagle without Marconi here? Get more information that way?"

Mariana had to stop a second, remembering that Umberto's last name was Marconi. "I hadn't thought about it. I can't do it here in the bar. I'll try tomorrow, though, and let you know if anything comes through."

"Why wouldn't his guide have stopped him from getting murdered?"

"Maybe he tried—maybe that was why Umberto said he was told to come for a reading. But people still have free will. Umberto also said that he had made up his mind what he was going to do. That's ego in the way again. The guided information either doesn't come through or for some reason doesn't send us in the direction we would consider right. Or it comes through and people do something else anyway." Mariana shrugged her shoulders. "Or maybe the murder was karma."

"Karma. That's fate, right?"

"Something like that, but only in the sense that what goes around, comes around, is fate. In physics, the law is, for every action there's an equal and opposite reaction. In metaphysics, it's as ye sow, so shall ye reap. The same thing. With karma, though, what went around, what ye sowed, could have happened in an earlier incarnation."

Claybourne laughed. "So you're telling me that somebody might have murdered Marconi for what he did in a past life?"

"I didn't say you have to believe me. And that doesn't mean the murderer shouldn't be brought to justice in this one."

"I'm glad to hear that." He was still chuckling over the idea. "Especially since your friend assured me earlier that I'll find the murderer."

"Perhaps stumble over the murderer," Mariana said, remembering the words. "And that might be a cosmic joke."

"How so?"

"I don't know." She felt a chill as she said it.

"You really believe in all this, don't you?"

"Karma? Past lives? Of course."

"How do you know you have past lives?" he asked.

"Because I dream about them," she said, and this time the chill made her shiver noticeably.

Claybourne's energy shifted, too. He took a final sip of wine. "Time to go."

Mariana nodded. She wanted to say something to lift the mood again, but the words weren't there.

"I guess you would have told us if you had any other leads on the murder," was the best she could come up with.

"I might have," he answered. "We didn't find anything in his apartment that helped, but we're still sifting through his things. We did confirm he worked for the county, but no one there seems to know much about him. The space in his personnel file on who to notify in case of emergency was blank. And there's still no sign of that woman you said you spoke to on the porch."

He looked at her expectantly, but she didn't have anything to add. She finished her wine and stood up.

"Come again," the bartender called out.

The young waiter held the door for them.

"Come again soon," he echoed.

Claybourne put a hand on Mariana's shoulder to stop her from walking into the street. "Look both ways," he said.

A car turned the corner and zipped past.

"Thanks. I don't do that often," she replied.

His hand stayed on her shoulder as they crossed to the car. She moved away, circling to the passenger side. It occurred to her that married men sometimes touch women too easily.

They took the short trip back to the store in silence. Silence was comfortable with Claybourne, Mariana thought. One of his likable qualities.

Alora's car was still in the same spot.

"That's it, then, for tonight," Mariana said.

"If you're at all concerned about safety, I could follow you home," Claybourne said.

"I'm not concerned about my own safety."

"You're sure that isn't ego?"

"Almost."

Claybourne started to reach over and touch her, then returned his hand to the steering wheel.

"Someone will have to officially report Alora missing," he said.

"I'll talk to Deirdre about that tomorrow." Mariana opened the car door. She stopped and added, "You know, even if you don't believe in past lives, the dreams work as metaphors. They help, they really do."

Claybourne looked dubious.

"Goodnight," Mariana said, getting out of the car.

"Goodnight. Call me if anything comes to you, even if you don't think it will help."

Mariana nodded. "I will."

Claybourne waited until she had started her car before he drove away. She could feel his eyes on her, even after he had left the parking lot.

And then she wasn't certain that they were his eyes that she felt.

But no one was there.

She drove home as quickly as she could, finally feeling safe when she had double locked the door and crawled into bed with her cats.

Darkness. Then, slowly, glimmers of light, but not real light, light from eyes. She could see eyes, eyes staring at her from the darkness, too many eyes to count.

She struggled to focus on what—who—was behind the eyes, but nothing came to her.

Only the eyes.

Chapter Ten

"I can't believe you're going ahead with the psychic fair," Mariana said. "One person was murdered and one has disappeared. Here at the store. How can we have a psychic fair?"

She had come to Enchantment on Sunday in response to Deirdre's call, asking her to fill in behind the counter for the missing Alora. The midmorning phone call had awakened her from a restless sleep, probably the result of the late-night glass of wine, and she was feeling irritable. She arrived to find Deirdre taping a flier to the glass front door.

"What do you expect me to do? Close the store? Of course I'm going ahead," Deirdre told her. "It's too late to cancel the ads in the *Ventura Weekly,* and the coupon clipper with the half-price for a second reading offer will be in mailboxes Wednesday. Besides, I wouldn't dream of disappointing Jerry. He is dying—his words—to see what he can pick up, and he and Ramon will be seeing the store for the first time, so I want to know what they sense, too. Truthfully, don't you?"

"I'll have to think about it." Mariana had mixed feelings about Jerry and Ramon, two psychics she had met during the same chaotic time when she had come to know Deirdre. "At least the day won't be dull. Is Mickey coming too?"

"No. He and Karella have Angelo with them now—Karella's ex gave up the custody battle—and they offered to take Jimmy and Caitlin for the weekend, bless them."

Mickey, Deirdre's brother, had been part of the same channeling group. Mariana's experience with him hadn't been a pleasant one. She was so relieved she wouldn't have to deal with him that she had to handle a pang of guilt. But relief won. Karella was Mickey's significant other, and Mariana would have liked seeing her under different circumstances, if only to ask what she was doing still with Mickey.

"So we're going to have four psychics working?" she asked.

"Six," Deirdre replied. "Jerry and Ramon are bringing two friends from the Valley. You can have the reading room, Jerry and Ramon get the two offices, and I'll set up card tables and partitions in the classroom to share with the others. Samantha was going to work the counter with Alora. If Alora isn't here, she'll just have to work it alone."

"I hope all of this works," Mariana said. When Deirdre just smiled, she added, "Did you call to report Alora missing?"

"I did. And I discovered how little I actually know about her. No legal name, no relatives. I also called both Samantha and Jeff, but neither one could add anything."

"Wouldn't it make more sense for Jeff to work, rather than for Samantha to be behind the counter by herself?" Mariana asked.

"Only if Jeff were good at handling crowds. He isn't. It's all he can do to focus on one person at a time. Anyway, he seems to think that Alora will turn up."

"Maybe she will." Mariana didn't feel as confident as Jeff was. "And there may be something in her apartment that will help us figure out what happened. Claybourne will probably get a warrant and search it tomorrow." She looked past Deirdre into the store. "What do you want me to do today?"

"Wait on customers and answer the phone while I'm reading. I have two scheduled, and I could have cancelled them, but I hate doing that." Deirdre grimaced and added, "I owe you one."

"That makes coming in worthwhile," Mariana replied.

"Why Claybourne?" Deirdre asked.

"What?"

"Your friend Claybourne wouldn't normally investigate a missing person report. What makes you think he'll take this one?"

"He isn't my friend." Mariana felt her face flush as she said it. "And I think he'll do it because he was here when it happened, and both Umberto's murder and Alora's disappearance are connected by the store and the channeling."

"Then maybe he'll look for your brother while he's at it," Deirdre said. She had finished taping the fliers. The look on her face was innocent, but Mariana didn't trust it. Deirdre was not as guileless as she liked to appear.

"What does Brian have to do with this?"

"The store and the channeling. And you."

"Maybe." Mariana wasn't comfortable with the thought. "But Umberto and Alora were alike in not having close ties to other people. Brian did."

"Did he? To whom?" Deirdre still looked innocent.

Mariana struggled to find a calm answer. Of course, Deirdre was right. Brian had cut his ties to everyone before he dropped out of sight. At least he had cut the ties Mariana knew about.

"Put your things down, and I'll show you how to record sales and figure the tax on the cash register," Deirdre said, once it was clear that Mariana had no ready reply to her question. "That's the only thing you need to know that you don't already."

Mariana followed Deirdre into the store. She placed her

bag in one of the large drawers behind the counter and listened to Deirdre's instructions.

The cash register was simple enough. The codes for the various items were written on a card taped to the side, and one key added the sales tax.

A woman in her sixties with heavily rouged cheeks and bleached blonde hair swept into curls on top of her head walked in as Deirdre was finishing.

"Hilda is my twelve-thirty appointment," Deirdre said. "Do you think you'll be okay?"

"I'll be fine," Mariana answered.

Deirdre greeted the older woman and ushered her back to the reading room.

Mariana looked around at the quiet store. Something was missing, and it took her a moment to realize what it was.

And then she did something that she never did in her apartment. She decided to put music on. Deirdre always had background music playing in the store, but today she had neglected to pick out a CD before Hilda arrived.

The collection was more extensive than Mariana had suspected. Deirdre believed that the soothing sounds of the CDs designed for Reiki practitioners made people want to stay in the store, so she rarely chose to play anything else. Mariana considered chants, drums, and nature sounds before opting for a Celtic soprano.

The echoes of ancient bards touched her spirit. She closed her eyes to listen.

"Mariana, you're here!"

She opened them again.

Art was leaning over the counter toward her. He was wearing the same clothes he had been wearing the night before, rumpled as if he had slept in them.

"Art. What are you doing here?" Mariana realized she

would have to work to keep a tight rein on her irritability.

"I called your apartment, and you weren't there, and I was too worried to stay home. Something is wrong, Mariana, I know it. I drove out to talk with Deirdre." The furrows on his forehead underscored his words.

"Well, yes, something is wrong, but I'm fine. Alora disappeared after the channeling. That's why I'm working today." She examined his face, wondering if he had slept at all. "Maybe talking with Deirdre would be a good idea. She'll be free in a few minutes."

Deirdre was a neutral party. She might be able to tune in to Art's stress in a way that Mariana couldn't, maybe even help him release it. Deirdre might be able to explain how he could use his psychic ability without draining his energy. Then, too, Deirdre might be able to convince Art to go home and stay home.

Art stepped back, shaking his head.

"I was sure it was you," he said. "I dreamed that I saw a woman swallowed by darkness, right outside this store, and I was sure it was you. But it wasn't like an ordinary dream—this one seemed real. I had to come here, find out what had happened."

"I guess I might have a superficial resemblance to Alora," Mariana said, reluctant to admit it. "At least the long dark hair. You had a vision, and you interpreted it through your own fears. That's easy to do. What else did you see?"

"That was all. I couldn't see what happened."

"You said swallowed. Swallowed how?"

Art shook his head again. "I had the sense of hands, grabbing her, but I couldn't see them. And Alora disappeared?"

"We couldn't find her last night after the channeling. Her car was still here this morning, and she didn't show up for work." While Mariana and Art were talking, a young woman in a pink tank top had come in, picked out a candle holder decorated with a metal butterfly and a round pink candle, and brought them to the counter. "Would you excuse me?"

Art nodded, and Mariana rang up the sale. She wrapped the candle and the holder in tissue paper, placed them in a white bag with the store's logo, and gave both package and change to the young woman.

"Alora isn't here?" the young woman asked.

"Not today," Mariana said, forcing a smile.

"I hope she's okay. She taught me a cool candle spell for love," the woman said. "Do you know any for money that I could use?"

"Burn a green candle, affirming prosperity as your divine right," Mariana said. That was the short version, but Mariana had come to the conclusion that the intention mattered more than the ritual. If rituals always worked, everyone would practice magic.

"Wait a sec while I get a green candle." The young woman wound her way back to the candle display, picked a green one, and came back. This time she counted out exact change.

"Thank you," Mariana said.

She and Art watched in silence until the young woman left the store.

"Try asking for a dream tonight," Mariana turned her attention back to Art. "See if you can get clarification. If you do get anything useful, Claybourne will want to know about it."

"What will I want to know?"

Mariana looked over to see the detective standing in the doorway.

"Art had a vision of a woman swallowed by darkness. He thought it was me, but it had to have been Alora."

"Unless it hasn't happened yet," Art said sharply. "I'm not convinced you're right."

"Then talk to Deirdre," Mariana responded just as sharply. "She'll be out of her reading any minute."

The tension level in the store had risen abruptly.

"What kind of vision?" Claybourne asked.

"Like a dream, but too strong for that," Art answered. "I really thought it was happening."

"It was. It was second sight, not clairvoyance. It has already happened, but it was Alora, not me." Mariana said sharply.

"Or you're denying you might be in danger," Art replied.

"And it wouldn't be the first time." Deirdre was approaching the counter. "Hello, Art. Hello, Claybourne. Could you all keep your voices down while customers are in the store?"

"I'm sorry," Mariana said.

They were all quiet while Deirdre took the payment for the reading and said good-bye to her client.

"Art, come with me," Deirdre said. She took his hand and led him back to the reading room.

"Why aren't you taking the warnings seriously?" Claybourne asked.

"I don't know." Mariana met his eyes. She felt comfortable whenever she looked into his eyes. And then the feeling bothered her, so she looked away. "I guess because I don't feel in danger, or at least I don't feel it most of the time. And I think I'd have some kind of warning."

"Deirdre said something about another time. What did she mean?"

Mariana grimaced. "I wish she hadn't mentioned that. There were some fatal accidents around me last year. The first happened to my husband. And I wasn't in trouble, or not at first, anyway, but a lot of people I knew, and Deirdre knew, were. I refused, for as long as I could, to believe that something without a rational explanation was going on, or that I

130

could do something to stop it. Then I had an out-of-body experience with an archangel during an earthquake."

She watched him struggle with his disbelief.

"I know," she continued, "I have trouble with it, too, and it happened to me. Sometimes I think it was only a vision, but Deirdre says it was real. Anyway, the difference now is that this time I'm willing to do anything I can to help, on whatever level. I think."

Mariana managed to smile at her own confusion.

"I'm sorry about your husband," Claybourne said. His face was soft with compassion.

"Thank you. But I'm pretty much all right about it now. I'm at least past the hysterical grief." She tried to keep her smile, then let it go. "That came out heavier than I intended."

"There's no statute of limitations on grief." Claybourne offered a gentle smile of his own. "I see a lot of it."

"And you've experienced some."

"My father died a few months ago. How can you tell?"

"I told you. I'm an empath. I can feel your pain—literally, if I'm not careful."

"Can I try on that ring?" Another young woman in tank top and jeans, almost identical to the earlier one, caught Mariana's attention from the end of the counter.

Mariana excused herself from Claybourne and moved down to help. "Which ring?"

"That one."

One ring turned into several. By the time Mariana had rung up the sale, Claybourne was no longer in sight. She opened her mouth to say his name, then shut it again. Calling him Claybourne didn't seem right, but she couldn't bring herself to call him David. She wanted another name.

She found him browsing in the book section. He had a book on creative dreaming in his hands, but put it down when he saw her.

"I thought I'd take a look at the White Eagle books as long as I was here," he said. "You're right. They don't help."

"He seems to have bowed out. I asked for a message from White Eagle in this morning's meditation. I didn't get one. Is White Eagle why you came here?" she asked.

"No." Clear hazel eyes met hers. Then he added, "I checked the computer this morning and found that Deirdre had filed a missing person's report. I wanted to follow up myself. Have either of you come up with anything?"

"Art's vision of hands from the darkness is more than either Deirdre or I have seen," Mariana said. "But you might want to wait a few minutes, just to see if Deirdre can tune in to something more concrete."

"Okay."

"And you didn't need to put the dream book back. Are you interested in dreams?"

"A little." He picked up the book again. "I rarely remember mine, but I know I have them. You mentioned past life dreams last night, and then today I was struck by the way your friend described his."

Deirdre saw Claybourne as her friend, Claybourne saw Art as her friend. Mariana wondered about that, about who her friends were. That was an unhealed wound, she knew, left over from the circumstances of Tim's death.

"I think Art's dream was more properly a vision, but the distinction isn't a firm one," she said.

They looked at each other. She was caught again by the familiarity of his hazel eyes, and she wished she could remember the name she wanted to call him. Not David, she knew that. But what?

"Could you read for me? Do something with your cards?" he asked.

"No. I mean, maybe I could, but I'd rather not try. It would be better if you had a stranger read for you, someone who isn't part of this." Mariana could feel herself blushing, and she hurried on. "Next Saturday we're having a psychic fair, Deirdre made fliers, and you could come back then. One of the others could read for you."

He nodded.

"I have to get back to the front of the store," she added.

"You do," he agreed. "Someone is at the counter, and I didn't mean to keep you."

The woman at the counter was waving a package of incense in Mariana's direction, clearly annoyed at having to wait. Mariana rang up the sale and the woman left without her receipt. Mariana crumpled it up and tossed it in the trash. She hadn't been away from the counter for that long, and the woman's attitude irritated her.

She looked for something to keep herself busy, and to keep herself away from Claybourne. Picking out another CD was all she could come up with. She settled on what turned out to be the mournful sounds of Native American flutes.

"By the way, I stopped by to see Marconi's neighbors again." Claybourne had followed her to the counter. "A young couple, just as the landlord said. They couldn't tell us anything we didn't already know. And they don't know who the old woman was, the one you spoke with."

"I'll go back there tomorrow," Mariana said, frowning.

"Be careful."

"I'm really tired of hearing that," Mariana said.

"Too bad." The voice was Deirdre's. She and Art were making their way along the aisle between crystals and incense. "Because you're probably going to hear it a lot more. I think Art's vision was right on. You were the target last night —Alora was grabbed by mistake."

She stood on the grass, just beyond the steps to the temple. The white marble columns formed a circle around a statue of the goddess, wearing a gown that rippled as if the figure moved through the winds of the world.

She was alone. Where were the others? The priestesses? Where were the women of her tribe?

Chapter Eleven

"I think you're both wrong." Mariana said it as calmly as she could. With the three of them looking at her as if she might drop off the edge of a cliff any moment, it was hard to maintain her composure. "Why would anyone want to grab me?"

"Why would anyone want to grab Alora?" Deirdre countered. "We don't know what's going on here. But all of us think that the body of the man who was murdered was intentionally dropped on our doorstep. You were the person who read for him. And there's no reason Art would have a vision about Alora."

"We have to talk about how you're going to protect yourself," Claybourne said.

"White light and angel shields," Mariana said. "That's working so far."

"I'd prefer something a little more concrete." Claybourne sounded stern and flat and something about the tone of his voice made Mariana want to pull away from him.

"So would I," Art added.

"Well, what would you suggest?" Mariana asked.

"Would you consider staying with someone until we found out more about what's going on?" Claybourne asked.

"No. I have two locked doors between me and the street, and I'd be willing to have you check the locks. But my apartment feels safe to me, and I'm happier there. So are the cats."

135

She felt a shiver as she said it. She hoped she was right.

"I could sleep on your couch," Art said.

"Absolutely not. Having you there would drain me, and your fear would confuse the energy—which I think is what's happening anyway," Mariana said. Something was draining her energy, and even though she could refuel, it was hit and miss. She would have to think what the energy drain might be.

"Will you at least promise that you won't wander around by yourself?" Claybourne asked.

"I promise I won't go out at night by myself," Mariana said. That was safe. She didn't do that much under any circumstances.

"If everyone can live with that," Deirdre said, "I'll ask to be excused. My next client is here. I'll also ask that you all be mindful of the store's customers."

"And keep our voices down," Mariana finished.

"Thank you." Deirdre nodded to her and turned away.

Mariana and the two men watched in silence as Deirdre greeted a white-haired man wearing a stained polo shirt that barely covered his apple-shaped belly and led him down the aisle toward the reading room. The man had such a worried expression on his face that he probably wouldn't have paid attention to anything short of a fire.

"Art, please go home," Mariana said. "I appreciate your concern. There's nothing you can do to help. Claybourne, go back to investigating. The sooner you get this solved, the sooner everyone will stop worrying about me."

Mariana looked from one to the other. Neither one moved, neither wanted to be the first to go.

Before she could decide on her next step, the telephone rang, and she had to turn away to answer.

"Who is this?" a woman's voice asked.

"Mariana. May I help you?"

"Oh, Mariana. It's Alora. Can I talk to Deirdre?"

"Alora! Where are you? We've been so worried! Deirdre's in a reading, you'll have to talk to me." Mariana felt a quick surge of relief that was immediately replaced by anger. She hoped Alora had a good explanation.

"I'm with some friends. Tell Deirdre I'm sorry I didn't call earlier to let her know I couldn't come in today. I'll be in on Tuesday, and I'll talk to her then."

There were voices in the background. Alora muffled the receiver, and Mariana could hear her talking with someone on the other end, but she couldn't make out the words.

"Alora, I need to know more than that," Mariana began, but the click in her ear advised her that Alora had hung up.

"What'd she say?" Claybourne asked. When he heard the name, he had moved in closer to eavesdrop. Art was right next to him.

"That she's fine and she'll be in on Tuesday," Mariana told him. "I'm sorry. You asked last night if she might have gone off with friends, and Deirdre and I said no, but we were both wrong. I guess we inconvenienced you on a Sunday for nothing."

"No, you had a right to be worried," Claybourne answered. "I'll stop by on Tuesday to talk with her, maybe shake her up a little for behaving so irresponsibly."

"Okay. Thanks."

Claybourne hesitated as if he might want to say something more, then waved his hand at her and left.

"I don't understand," Art said. "Do you really think she's all right?"

"Yes. I think we've all been flying along the wrong air lane. That happens, you know." Mariana reached out for his shoulder. "Art, that doesn't mean your vision was wrong. It just means you interpreted it through your own fears. Alora left with friends, unexpectedly. She was snatched away, but it wasn't a kidnapping. Really."

Art shook his head. He took her hand in both of his. "I'm not convinced it can be explained away that easily. If I stay until evening, could I talk you into having dinner?"

"No. I'm tired, and I want to be alone this evening. But thank you." Mariana said it so firmly that he didn't argue.

"Will you keep in touch?"

"If I don't, I'm sure you will." That came out a little harsher than she intended, but she didn't try to take it back. "Good-bye."

"Good-bye."

Art dragged his way out the door.

Mariana turned back to the file of CDs on the shelf against the wall. There was something she wanted to hear, but she wasn't quite certain what it was. She began to search the stacks, touching each one.

Something with chanting, she wanted something with chanting. She picked a Krishna Das CD that felt almost right. As the call and response *Om Namah Shivaya* began, she closed her eyes to listen. The second selection was one she didn't know, but the third cut was *Hare Krishna,* and she softly joined her voice to the chorus.

"Did they leave?" Deirdre's words interrupted her concentration. Mariana turned around to see the apple-bellied man walking out the door and Deirdre slipping behind the counter.

"Yes. And Alora called to say she's all right, and she'll see you on Tuesday."

"Where is she?" Deirdre's eyebrows shot up in surprise. Her eyes were set so deeply that it was normally hard to see their color, but at that moment they appeared as a startlingly bright green.

Mariana was distracted by Deirdre's eyes. She would have to think about eyes, why they were so important lately.

"She said she's with friends. She didn't want to talk with me," Mariana said. "In fact, she hung up. It seems we were way off on this."

"Maybe. Or maybe Alora lied to you," Deirdre said.

"What do you mean? She sounded fine."

"Well, yes, fine now, anyway."

"You just don't want to admit you were wrong," Mariana said.

"Under other circumstances, I'd agree with you. This time, I don't think we know the whole story. Why don't we let it drop until Tuesday and see what she tells me?" Deirdre smiled. "If you like, I'll call you and let you know."

"I won't argue. And yes, I would like to know what she says. Claybourne said he'd stop by to growl at her for worrying us, by the way."

"And he may let you know what her story is before I do."

"Deirdre, stop it. There's nothing between us. Really. And there isn't going to be." Mariana found her voice faltering, though. She looked around the empty store. "Is there something I can do to be useful?"

"Polish jewelry." Deirdre reached under the counter and picked up a polishing glove, which she handed to Mariana. "You can start with the heavy silver pieces in the far case. And you can dust the brass Hindu gods."

Mariana took the glove, pulled the stool down to the end of the counter, opened the case, and started work.

The heavy silver pieces were hand-wrought pendants embedded with semi-precious stones, opal and amethyst and topaz. They were eye-catching, especially when polished, but they always struck Mariana as too gaudy to wear.

"I saw something on television the other night, that observant Hindus are upset about the way their religious symbols are used decoratively," Mariana said. "They ought to be upset about the way we carelessly discuss Hindu gods."

"I thought Krishna said something about it not mattering how you worship, as long as you worship," Deirdre answered.

"And there's something in the Upanishads about the One appearing as Many, indicating that the small-g gods may not be all that different from Jungian archetypes," Mariana said.

"Must you bring everything back to Jung?" Deirdre sighed.

"No. I just like the idea that everything can be connected to everything else," Mariana said.

"Will you pardon me while I connect some books to an invoice?" Deirdre asked.

Mariana put her head down and polished.

A few customers wandered in and out, and Deirdre had one more reading, but all in all the rest of the afternoon passed quietly.

It wasn't until the next morning, after another restless night, that Mariana realized that one of the voices that Alora had muffled had sounded familiar.

A woman's voice, but whose? She hadn't heard the words, so all she had was a sense of the tone, a vague sense of the speaker. Who? Another unanswered question, along with who murdered Umberto, where was Brian, and what happened to the old woman who had talked to her from the porch next to Umberto's.

That one, however, she might be able to do something about.

On Monday afternoon, Mariana drove back along Harbor Boulevard past the strawberry fields and the power plant perched in the wetlands to the faded community where

Umberto had lived. The sky was gray from a low cloud cover, which looked as if it wasn't going to burn off.

The yellow tape across the porch meant that the police hadn't yet finished with the apartment. Mariana walked up to the adjacent porch, past the potted jade plant, and knocked on the door. When no one came, she knocked again.

"I don't think I can help you."

It was the old woman's voice, but the door hadn't opened.

Mariana craned her neck to the upstairs window. She could barely make out the face.

"I'd like to talk with you anyway," she said. "Why did you hide from the police?"

"Who says I hid?"

"The detective. He said you wouldn't answer the door. And then he talked to a young couple who told him you don't live here."

The face blurred even more, then became firm as the woman leaned closer to the screen. "I do live here. But I'm not on the lease, that's all."

Mariana thought of how cramped Umberto's place had seemed. Three people couldn't fit comfortably, even without the garbage and the clutter, and she could understand that a landlord might not approve.

"I promise not to tell, then," she said. "Whatever information you give, I won't say it came from you."

"No information. I don't know anything more than I already told you about Bert."

Mariana squinted, trying to see the woman's eyes. "Are you sure there isn't anything you know about Bert that could help find out who killed him? You're here so much, you must have seen people come and go. Or maybe he said something to you."

"He said he wanted to move, but I didn't think he wanted

to die. My daughter didn't think so, either, and she's psychic like Bert. Are you psychic too?"

Mariana hesitated, then said, "Yes. I work as a psychic. And I didn't think he wanted to die, either. What's your name?"

"Hannah Jane." The woman's face blurred and came back into focus. "If you want, you can come another time. I'll try to think of something more."

Hannah Jane backed away from the window and disappeared.

"Thank you, Hannah Jane," Mariana called, but there was no response.

Mariana walked back to her car, frowning, trying to decide what she could tell Claybourne without violating Hannah Jane's confidence about the lease situation. Nothing really. The woman hadn't said anything except what Mariana already knew, that Umberto had wanted to move. And that she had a psychic daughter. We're taking over the world, Mariana thought. But Hannah Jane wasn't likely to volunteer information to Claybourne. So there wasn't any point in telling Claybourne about her unless he brought her up, which didn't seem likely.

The only two things Mariana's little excursion had confirmed were that the old woman did live next door, even though she had avoided the police, and that the old woman's voice was not the one on the telephone. That voice had been younger, Mariana was certain—not a lot younger, but not that old.

She wondered how long it would take to eliminate every woman's voice she had ever heard until she found the right one. Too long. She would have to wait until she heard it again.

Mariana knew she would hear the voice again. A small

chill rippled through her body, then disappeared as she started her car.

The rest of Monday passed uneventfully. On Tuesday, Deirdre turned out to be right about one more thing. Claybourne called to tell her Alora's story.

"She insisted that two friends were waiting for her in the parking lot to take her to a party, and that when she left in their car, it didn't occur to her that anyone would worry about her. She said the party ran late, she had a few drinks and stayed over. She woke in the morning with a hangover and didn't make it to work." There was a strong note of skepticism in the detective's voice.

"You don't believe her," Mariana said.

"No. But she appears to be fine, so there's nothing I can do about it."

"Deirdre thought she was lying, too. Maybe Deirdre can get a better story out of her."

"Maybe."

"I'll talk to her later. If she does add anything, I'll call you." She wanted to ask if he had any new leads on Umberto's murder, but stopped herself. He might then ask her, and she didn't want to talk about Hannah Jane.

"Okay. And Mariana, I still think you should be careful. Stay close to your apartment and the store unless someone is with you. Even though Alora is okay. Understood?"

Mariana suppressed her annoyance. "I promised not to wander at night. I keep my promises."

After she hung up the phone, Mariana thought about Alora and her phantom friends. She disliked Alora too much to trust her own impulses, but with both Deirdre and Claybourne believing that Alora was lying, she felt all right agreeing with them. There had to be some way to check Alora's story. She wondered if it were possible that the two vampire children walking down the sidewalk across the street that night had seen anything. The only way to reach the vampire children that she could think of was through the small group that hung out on Thompson, the ones she and Art had seen on their way to dinner.

Walking to Thompson, less than half a block away, couldn't be considered wandering. But she would have to wait until nightfall, when the vampire children came out to play.

Deirdre called her shortly after five, once Alora had left for the day.

"Claybourne told me," Mariana said. "Alora insists she's fine, she was always fine, that she left with friends. He doesn't believe her story."

"I don't either, although she does seem to have found a new friend, a young man with a fondness for black clothes and pierced body parts," Deirdre said. "For now, though, I'm going to let it go. I still think you should be careful."

"You and Claybourne have the same scriptwriter."

"Or great minds think alike."

"I'll tell you the same thing I told him," Mariana said. "I won't wander alone at night."

"Good. Then I'll expect to see you Thursday."

Mariana was annoyed at both Deirdre and Claybourne when she hung up the phone.

She watched the sky until sunset, then slipped out of her apartment and down to the corner.

A battered pickup truck honked and slowed down.

She quickly retreated to her front door. Only when she was certain the truck driver had given up did she return to the corner. She hoped she wasn't invading someone's territory. She didn't know much about the reputed prostitution in that area, but the so-called hooker motel was in the next block.

Three more drivers tried to solicit her favors before Mariana decided to give up the vampire hunt for the night.

The next night she was successful, staying in the shadows until she saw a group of black-caped figures coming her way.

But when she stepped forward to talk with them, the white-faced young man who was leading the small procession pointed at her and started laughing. The three young women and the other young man started to point and laugh as well.

"Excuse me," Mariana began, but in response the laughter became louder.

"Excuse you?" the young man shrieked. "Excuse me!"

The others picked up the chorus.

"Excuse you?"

"Excuse you?"

"Excuse me!"

"Excuse me!"

Humiliated, Mariana ran back to her apartment.

The laughter followed her up the stairs. She heard it long into the night.

Her dark robes were heavy, and the shift she wore underneath was rough, scratching her skin. She could smell her own body in the folds of material.

She moved as quietly as she could along the corridor until she came to the door, left slightly ajar, and slipped inside.

He was standing at the window. He turned and held out his arms, the long sleeves reaching almost to the floor, almost as long as the skirted robe that looked so much like hers.

And she didn't leave his arms until the sky was becoming light.

No one caught them that night, or the next. But it happened. One morning three robed figures opened the door while she was asleep in his bed.

The day came that he was dead and she was disgraced and she lived the rest of her life alone.

Who . . .

Chapter Twelve

"That office is too hot," Jerry said, waving his hand in front of his face to emphasize his discomfort. "Don't you have air conditioning?"

"You might want to make an appointment to see Samantha. She can give you some evening primrose and wild yam, and more soy in your diet would help," Deirdre said with a smile. "And the air conditioning is on."

"I am not having hot flashes," Jerry snapped. "The office is hot and stuffy."

"Check the vents. Jeff may have closed them for some reason." Deirdre patted him on the shoulder and turned to Mariana. The three of them were standing at the back of the store, almost blocking the hall to the offices. Deirdre and Mariana had been watching the store fill with people when Jerry came to complain. "Are you set up yet? Your first appointment is in five minutes. Let Alora know before you start. She is booking the appointments, and Samantha is collecting the money and handing out the tickets. Red for thirty minutes, blue for fifteen minutes. Got it?"

Mariana nodded, keeping a wince about checking with Alora to herself. She wouldn't have believed that so many people could be squeezed into the small store. But there was clearly a market in Ventura for a psychic fair.

Mariana would rather have checked with Samantha.

Mariana was still annoyed with Alora, both for the fiasco of the weekend before and for the barely veiled hostility Alora had radiated for the last two days. Mariana had stayed out of her way as much as possible, a task made more difficult when she had only two readings on Thursday and none on Friday. Everyone had evidently waited for the low psychic fair rates.

"And your space is cool, I suppose," Jerry said to her. He was dressed in jeans and a red-and-yellow flowered Hawaiian shirt that, combined with a three-day growth of beard, gave him a kind of Hollywood-scruffy look.

"There's a fan in the reading room," Mariana said. "And with the air conditioning on, I won't need it. Why don't you take it for the afternoon?"

"Good thought," Deirdre said. "Now if you'll excuse me, Jerry, I want to make certain that your two friends are comfortable in the classroom."

"Where's that fan?" Jerry asked.

"This way." Mariana led him back to the reading room.

Jerry pulled the plug from the wall and wrapped the cord loosely around his hand.

"You didn't ever write that book, did you?" he asked.

"I don't remember saying I was going to write one."

Jerry smiled his court jester smile. "I think I said it, remember? I'll write it with you."

"Thank you for offering, but no," Mariana said firmly.

"There you are." Ramon leaned into the room. His dress was as casual as his partner's, a faded red *Justice for Janitors* sweatshirt over jeans. "Samantha says our first readings are here, and we ought to get started. Hello, Mariana."

"Hello, Ramon," Mariana said, but Ramon was already gone.

"See you later," Jerry said, hefting the fan. "Remember to breathe between readings."

Deirdre had offered the same advice. Mariana felt like the new kid on the block.

She started back down the hall, planning to dutifully check with Alora, then stopped at the sound of a woman's voice. It was the same one she had heard, muffled, when Alora had called to say she was fine.

Mariana paused at the edge of the hall to survey the store again.

Deirdre and Alora had decorated for autumn, with displays of brown and yellow leaves, some ears of dried corn, and a scattering of berries. The only concession to Halloween was a shiny black cat with its back arched and its green eyes wide, peeking out from behind a round, scraggly broom just inside the glass doors. Deirdre had decided to avoid the witches and the ghosts—too obviously occult for her tastes.

The aisles were crowded with some of the usual customers and some Mariana didn't remember seeing before. Stella and Bernard were there, probably because Stella wanted her weekly psychic fix, and Deirdre had cancelled the regular Saturday evening channeling because of the fair.

There were at least four women Mariana had read for, maybe more. She couldn't put names with two of the faces, which meant she hadn't seen them often. One had fuzzy black hair and bland features. The second was wearing a blond wig that seemed out of place with her lined face. Mariana wasn't comfortable with her vague memories of either of them.

The other two were women she knew well. Kim and Pauline, the two widows who shared the same philandering dead husband. They were glaring at each other across a crystal that had split into two even points, the kind known as a twin flame, the crystal equivalent of a soul mate.

"I believe I saw it first," Pauline said.

"You hadn't picked it up," Kim countered.

Of course both women would want it, Mariana thought. Each wants to believe her dead husband is her twin flame.

She started toward them, hoping to defuse the situation, when a short woman with flying gray hair bumped into her.

"Excuse me, Mariana honey," the woman said. Her glasses were held together on one side by a paper clip, and they didn't sit quite evenly on her nose. She adjusted them slightly to get a better look at Mariana. "I want to get started."

Trina. Jerry had introduced her as Trina, one of the two psychics he and Ramon had brought. Mariana decided that she was really going to make an effort with names. The way they sometimes flowed through her head, never attached to a face, would have to stop.

Trina straightened her long black dress, which was clinging a little too tightly to her round figure, and swept past. The woman following her had bright red hair and a tight over-made-up face. The look she gave Mariana made it clear that Mariana had read for her, and the woman hadn't been happy with the reading.

Mariana smiled and nodded and let them go.

"Mariana!" Samantha called from behind the counter. "Stella is waiting!"

"Thanks, Samantha," Mariana called back. She decided she would have to leave Kim and Pauline to resolve the crystal situation by themselves. "Tell Alora I'm starting, would you?"

Samantha nodded, and Mariana felt relieved of that burden.

Stella squeezed between Kim and an incense rack to get to where Mariana was standing.

"The prices are so low today," she said. "It had to be my guides telling me it was time to try another psychic. I love

Deirdre, of course, and I wouldn't miss a Baba-ji channeling, but it'll be good to hear another point of view. And I've noticed, the few times you've come to the channeling, how wonderful your energy is."

"I'll do my best," Mariana said, leading her to the reading room.

Stella gave Mariana one of the blue tickets that meant she had paid for fifteen minutes and settled into her chair.

"You know, we've been out of the commune for eight years, and I still appreciate the freedom to get a second opinion more than anything else," Stella said.

"Out of the commune?"

"Yes—didn't you know? Bernard and I lived in a commune for twenty years. The guru made all our decisions." Stella shook her head. "Twenty wasted years."

"Was it near here? Is it still going?"

Stella looked surprised. "I suppose it's still going. I don't know what you mean by near."

"Well—within an hour's drive."

"Maybe. Depending on how fast you drive. I'm not sure I want to talk about that, Mariana. I really want to ask about my son and his girlfriend."

"I'm sorry," Mariana said, embarrassed at having gone off on a tangent related to her own affairs. And there was no reason to suddenly think that Brian might be in a commune. Except that Stella had been there the night Baba-ji told her that a contact could help her find him. And when Stella said the word commune, Mariana had felt a slight chill. There was something she needed to know about the commune. But it would have to wait. "I haven't started your fifteen minutes yet. Let's do your reading, and maybe you could tell me about the commune another time."

Stella nodded. A little of the cheer had faded from her face.

Mariana shuffled the cards and visualized the hawk on her shoulder.

She didn't have much to tell Stella, except that her guides wanted her to shift her focus from her son to herself, to make some decisions about her own life, and Stella didn't seem to be able to hear that. And after Stella, there was another client waiting, and another after her, almost without pause.

By the end of the day, Mariana had done brief readings for twelve people, about what she would normally do in three days. Most were people she hadn't seen before—neither the woman with the fuzzy black hair nor the woman with the blond wig had booked with her.

Samantha had allowed time for breaks, and during the first two, Mariana had tried to listen for the voice of Alora's so-called friend, but after that, she had needed to take the time to center herself. Even so, by the time the last person left, she was feeling as if her brain had been coated with a layer of fuzz.

She sat by herself with her hands over her eyes, trying to find her own center.

"Time for dinner," Jerry said, poking his head in the reading room.

"I'm not sure I can make it," Mariana said, not bothering to look at him. "Anyway, I'm too tired to eat. My stomach is churning. I'm not even sure I can drive myself home."

"You look like a clogged toilet," Jerry said, "on an astral level, of course, not a physical one. You've been reading with your chakras flat open, taking in other people's problems through your solar plexus, and now you have to let them go. If you don't, you'll make yourself sick."

Mariana took her hands away from her eyes and blinked at

him, not certain what he was talking about. He squeezed around behind her chair and put his hands on her head.

"Visualize a psychic shower," he ordered. "Wash everything out of your body, all the crap you took in this afternoon." He paused, waiting for her to do as told. "Very good. Now close your chakras, not all the way, but enough to hold your own energy in."

The shower was easy. Closing chakras was harder— Mariana could feel her solar plexus chakra blazing like the sun at high noon, absorbing energy from her cells and turning it to light. But that particular inner light was eating her alive. She worked it down to a small yellow circle, fighting to keep it under control. Jerry's hands on her head helped to calm the energy spurts. After a few minutes of this, she began to feel calm and peaceful.

"Thank you," she said. "That helped."

"The least I could do. After all, you saved my life."

"Don't remind me of that night. Please. And let's call it even." Mariana gathered her cards, folded a cloth around them, and put them in her bag. She dropped the small clock she used to time readings on top and tucked her teacup along the side. Then she gathered up the red and blue tickets into a neat stack. "I'm ready."

"Too bad you couldn't save what's-his-name, the guy who was murdered here a couple of weeks ago." Jerry said it so cheerfully that the good will Mariana was starting to feel toward him dissipated immediately.

"We all have our limits," she said.

"I know we all want to hear anything you've picked up about the murder, Jerry." Deirdre was standing in the doorway, smiling at them. "But it can wait until we're out of here. Everyone okay?"

"If you mean me, I guess so," Mariana said. "I got spaced

out. And Jerry really did help me."

"Good. If you're both relatively grounded, why don't you cash out your tickets with Samantha and then join the others in front of the store so I can close up?" Deirdre asked. "Some of us are ready for dinner."

Jerry had to squeeze back out from behind the chair so that Mariana could push it away from the table. She followed him down the hall and through the store to the counter and waited while Samantha checked his tickets against her records.

"Everyone did well today," Samantha said. "We're off to a good start. I hope you know how much Deirdre appreciates it that you and Ramon and your friends came out to help her start the psychic fairs."

"Not that she's paying us what we're worth," Jerry answered, slipping the cash in his wallet. "But thank you."

"You're the last one," Samantha said to Mariana. "How did it go? You're looking a little off center."

"I feel a little off center," Mariana answered. "Jerry helped me clean chakras, but I'm not my usual perky self."

"What perky self? If you were perky, I'd call you into my office to see who the impostor was."

Mariana managed a smile. She exchanged her tickets for cash and put the money in her purse.

"Are you coming for dinner?" she asked.

"Wouldn't miss it. I'll just help Deirdre close up, and we'll meet you outside," Samantha replied. She hit the button on the cash register to add up the day's sales.

As soon as the tape stopped, Deirdre stepped in to tear it off. She barely glanced at the numbers before she folded it up and placed it in one of the drawers beneath the counter.

"We're done," she said. "Everybody out."

Mariana and Samantha were barely through the door

when Deirdre turned out the lights. She set the alarm and followed them.

The sun was already low in the sky, even though it wasn't yet six o'clock, and the warmth of the afternoon had dissipated. Mariana wished she had brought a jacket.

Mariana started toward the others, but then she noticed that Jerry and Ramon were smoking, and so were their two friends, Trina and the other one. Mariana stayed near the door, both to avoid the smoke and to concentrate on coming up with the psychic's name. Celie, that's what it was. Celie was the kind of thin that only looks good on models, not human beings. A long paisley shift fell straight to her ankles without pausing. She had short dark hair that curled around her face and deep-set eyes with circles under them so dark they could almost be bruises. She turned to look at Mariana, then seemed to look past her instead.

Mariana glanced back, but no one was behind her.

"It's all right," Celie whispered. "The spirit is a friendly one."

"I hope so," Mariana said with a sigh, still too tired to care very much. She became marginally more alert when she noticed that Alora was standing just past the group of psychics. And then she noticed Art was there, too.

Deirdre began giving directions to a restaurant, one of those chains with a salad bar and buffet so that there would be no problem with separate checks. Mariana waited until people were nodding and moving toward their cars.

"I thought it would be just the psychics and Samantha," she said.

"And Art and Alora. She worked today and I invited her to go with us. I couldn't very well exclude her. You don't have to sit next to her, you know. Or next to him, either. He showed up and was moping around after his reading, so I invited him, too," Deirdre said.

"His reading? Who read for him?"

"I'm not sure. You'll have to ask."

Mariana struggled with that for a moment.

"All right," she finally said. "I'll see you at the restaurant."

She was still feeling spaced out as she stepped off the curb to cross the parking lot. Under other circumstances, she would have skipped dinner. But she knew she needed to eat, and soon, to keep her body grounded. And she was too tired to contemplate cooking anything for herself.

Art was walking toward her, but she didn't want to talk with him, not then. She scooted between the two cars parked in front of the store and picked up her pace.

"Mariana!"

Art was dashing after her. He looked so desperate that she stopped, not certain what was going on.

"Mariana! No!"

He took a flying leap in her direction, and she stumbled away from him, almost falling.

The black car caught him in mid-leap.

Art bounced off the hood of the car, hitting it again before landing on his head and shoulder. The car sped away. Art's body twitched, then fell still, blood streaming from his nose.

Mariana could hear someone screaming. She had a vague sense that the voice was her own.

Something had gone wrong. The ship had dropped her in the water, and she couldn't see the shore. She struggled to stay afloat, but the water was cold and the sky was dark and she had no will to survive.

Chapter Thirteen

Samantha took charge. Mariana stood and watched, frozen to the spot, as Samantha knelt on the asphalt and checked the pulse in Art's neck. His head leaned toward his shoulder at an unnatural angle, and Samantha was careful not to disturb it. His body looked small and battered, and when a red glow fell across it from someone's taillights, for a moment it appeared blood-stained. Mariana had to shut her eyes to keep him from turning into her vision of Brian or her nightmare of Tim. She knew she should rush forward and offer help, but she couldn't move.

"He's still alive," Samantha said. "Everybody stay back. We don't know how badly he's hurt. Somebody call the paramedics."

"I've called 911," a man said, waving his cell phone. "An ambulance is on the way."

Mariana opened her eyes to see who was talking. She looked at the man without recognition. He wasn't part of their group, and it took her a moment to realize—thanks to the videotapes in his hands—that he had simply walked out of the video store just in time to witness the accident.

"It's happened again, hasn't it?" Jerry asked no one in particular. "Mariana has attracted another disaster, and here we are."

"Jerry, that's not fair," Deirdre said. "You can't blame this on Mariana. Give us all a break until Art gets to the hospital. And then we can talk about how the energy of this group, which includes you and Ramon, might have attracted a disaster."

"All right, but I can't wait that long for food. If anyone wants us, we'll be in the pizza place." Jerry started toward the fast food restaurant on the other side of the video store. When he realized no one except Ramon was following, he stopped and added, "I'll order enough for everyone. We all need to eat, you know."

"We'll get some beer and soda, too," Ramon said, "and bring everything to the store."

"I hope no one is blaming Mariana," Celie said, "but this wasn't an accident, and Mariana was the target. The friendly spirit, the one by the door, made sure she was out of the way."

"And someone here knows who was in the car," Trina added. "Mariana, you know. Who is trying to hurt you?"

Mariana sat down abruptly on the asphalt. Deirdre stood over her, protectively. People had come out of the stores, and a small crowd was gathering.

"I don't know who would want to hurt me, Trina," Mariana said. "I truly don't."

"I think you do," Trina insisted. "When I read for your friend Art, I received a clear message from the other side. That particular spirit has been communicating with Art because it couldn't get you to listen. You don't want to hear the message, dear, but that doesn't mean you don't intuitively know its content."

"What?" Mariana had lost track of the words.

"Not every spirit is wise, and not every spirit wishes us well," Deirdre said. "You may mean well, Trina, but that doesn't mean the spirit who has been talking to Art does. Art doesn't know the difference, but you should."

Deirdre reached down and took Mariana's arm.

159

"Come on," she said. "We're going back into the store."

Mariana made it to her feet, mostly because Deirdre was pulling. The two women crossed the parking lot to the store, Deirdre doing her best to shield Mariana from both Art's body and the curious watchers.

Deirdre turned off the alarm and turned on the lights.

"You can sit on the stool behind the counter," she said. "I'll get you a cup of tea."

Dutifully, Mariana slipped behind the counter.

"Please don't leave until Samantha gets here," she said. "I don't want to be alone with the others—Jerry may not be the only one who blames me."

Deirdre paused, halfway down the aisle, and came back. "If that means you're blaming yourself, stop it right now. We can talk about responsibility, and karmic lessons, and what we attract, but don't let Jerry lay any kind of guilt trip on you."

"Not even when Art was protecting me?"

"Not even when Art was protecting you. Art wanted to protect you. And he may yet be all right."

Neither one quite believed that. But Trina was coming through the door, Celie right behind her, and neither one wanted to continue the conversation.

"The ambulance is here," Trina said. "And your friend is still alive. That's a good sign."

"The friendly spirit is gone now," Celie added. "The spirit was only here to protect you."

"But it wasn't the same spirit that had a message for your friend Art," Trina said. "Or at least I don't think it was."

"Would you mind bringing some chairs from the classroom?" Deirdre asked. "When Jerry and Ramon arrive with the food, we'll need a place to sit. We can eat at the counter."

"Do I have to put up with them?" Mariana snapped, as

soon as she thought the women were out of earshot.

"Only for a little while. The police will need to talk with them. And we all need to eat, Jerry was right about that." Deirdre paused, frowned, then continued. "But I don't think you have to put up with Alora. I haven't seen her since the accident."

"Tell me what you did see," Mariana said.

"I wasn't looking in your direction until I heard Art shout. I saw him push you out of the way, and a speeding black car hit him. The car swerved and kept going. I'm not going to make a good witness for the police," Deirdre said.

"It's eight of us, is that right?" Trina called from the hallway.

"Only seven," Deirdre answered. "The six psychics and Samantha."

"Well, we brought eight chairs anyway." Trina bustled into the store with two folding chairs under each arm, with Celie trailing behind. "We thought it was eight."

"What happened to the strange girl?" Celie asked.

"Strange girl? You mean Alora?" Deirdre replied.

"The one who was working behind the counter with Samantha," Celie said, leaning the chairs against the jewelry case. "I can't remember her name."

"Why did you think she was strange?" Mariana asked.

"Because of her energy. She sucks it in. Most people who work in metaphysical stores give it out," Celie answered. "And because I couldn't remember her name, no matter how many times I checked with her to see who was next. I kept blocking her name."

"Did either of you see the driver of the car?" Deirdre asked. She began unfolding the chairs and setting them in the aisle.

Mariana glanced at her, knowing she had intentionally

changed the subject.

"It was too dark," Trina said. She was still burdened by her chairs and seemed unsure how to get rid of them until Deirdre took them away from her. "But I think there was more than one person."

"You didn't see that," Celie said. "We couldn't really see anything."

"Tell me what happened when you read for Art," Mariana said.

"Oh, honey, I feel so bad," Trina said, shaking her head. Her glasses bobbled, and she had to straighten them out again. She sat down in one of the chairs that Deirdre had set up. "I knew it was a challenging time for him, and for you too, of course, but I just didn't see that car coming."

"Does anyone besides Mariana want tea?" Deirdre asked.

"I'll wait for a soda," Trina said.

Celie shook her head.

"Where's Samantha?" Mariana asked.

"On her way," Deirdre said. "And I want tea."

Mariana glared, but Deirdre left anyway.

"This has to be so terrible for you, Mariana honey," Trina said. "Art loves you so much, even though you don't love him, and he was so worried, with his nightmares and everything. And I just hate it that I didn't realize disaster was so close."

"There are no accidents, you know that," Celie said. "The spirit stood guard to make certain that you were safe and Art was in the way of the car, because that was the will of the Lords of Karma. If we had been supposed to warn you, we would have."

Mariana felt her anger rising. She didn't want to risk speaking, so she hugged herself tightly and nodded in turn at each of the women. She was saved from further response by

Samantha's entrance.

"The ambulance has left," Samantha said as she came through the doors. "I told the paramedics we would follow them to the hospital. Art's still alive, but barely."

"We?" Mariana asked.

"Of course. You knew him better than anyone here, and someone has to talk to the hospital staff. And I'm not letting you drive yourself over and deal with the situation alone." Samantha stood poised to leave again. "The police are here, talking with anyone who saw anything. I told them you and I were going to the hospital, and that the other psychics would wait in the store."

"Samantha, I need to put something in my stomach first. Please sit, just for a minute, just for a cup of tea, a fast cup of tea, and then we'll go," Mariana pleaded. She wondered if the officers were the same ones who had come when Umberto was killed. If so, she would rather not talk with them. They were only going to laugh at the psychics for missing what had happened in front of the store for a second time. She wanted to talk to Claybourne.

"Have a slice of pizza, too," Trina said to her. "You can cope better with anything after a little food."

"The tea is a good idea," Samantha said, "but whoever decided on pizza has a poor sense of the nutritional needs of the human body under stress. A lot of fat is not the best choice. But I guess it's better than nothing."

"And it's fast," Jerry added. He and Ramon had arrived with two pizza boxes and a bag of drinks just in time to hear Samantha's remark.

"The organic fruit stands were simply too far to drive," Ramon said, pulling a six-pack of beer and another of Coke out of the bag and placing them on the counter. "Besides, whatever you say about fat nutritionally, fat comforts and fat grounds. Right now, we need comfort and grounding."

He slipped a beer can from its plastic ring and popped the top.

"Cheers," he added and took a gulp.

"I'll grant you fat, but alcohol doesn't ground," Samantha said.

"Then don't drink it," Jerry said, reaching for a beer can. "And you're welcome."

"I'm grateful, Jerry. It was thoughtful of you to bring food for all of us," Trina said. "But I'll stick with Coke."

"Of course we're grateful," Celie said. "Are the pizzas vegetarian?"

"One is, one isn't," Jerry said with a sigh.

"What about plates and napkins?" Trina asked.

"Right here." Deirdre placed a stack of paper plates and napkins on the counter. Two cups of tea were precariously balanced on top.

Mariana rescued one of the cups.

"Samantha and I are going to the hospital," she said. "But before we go, did anyone pick up anything helpful?"

She hit the word helpful a little too hard, and Trina glared at her.

"Look both ways, Mariana," Celie said. "Look both ways."

"That's supposed to be helpful?" Jerry asked.

"Art's spirit is floating above his body," Ramon said. "If you want to see him while he's alive, you might want to leave now."

Mariana felt her stomach lurch.

"Bring the tea with you," Samantha said. "And pizza if you want. I'll drive."

Deirdre put two pieces of the vegetarian pizza on a plate and handed it to Mariana, with napkins.

"One for each of you," she said. "Go. We'll talk when you get back."

Mariana put her bag over her arm, and with tea in one hand and paper plate in the other, she followed Samantha out the door.

The two women rode to the hospital in silence. Mariana nibbled a little of the pizza, but her stomach didn't want to accept it.

Samantha found a parking place close to the emergency entrance.

"I'm not going to be able to eat this," Mariana said. "Do you want me to leave it for you?"

"No. Anyone who can eat that has a stomach of steel," Samantha answered.

Mariana dumped the plate with the pizza into the trash receptacle near the hospital door.

They went inside and identified themselves to a receptionist.

Art's wallet had provided much of the information that the hospital needed. Mariana was able to offer only a little more —she knew Art had a brother who lived in Downey, although she had never met him.

She and Samantha settled into plastic bucket chairs to wait.

"Can I get you something from the cafeteria?" Samantha asked. "Soup?"

"I'll try soup," Mariana told her. "Thank you."

Samantha left, returning a few moments later with two cups of soup and another two of tea on a small tray.

The soup turned out to be cream of broccoli, and Mariana ate that and drank the tea. Her stomach began to relax a little.

The police officers arrived before they had a chance to talk with the doctor treating Art.

It was the same two, but to Mariana's relief, they weren't laughing this time. The male officer went off to find medical information about Art, and the female officer sat down beside Mariana.

"Just tell us what you saw with your own two physical eyes," the female officer said. She sounded so weary that Mariana was certain the woman had heard enough visions for one day.

"Nothing helpful," Mariana answered. "I was crossing the parking lot, Art yelled at me, I stopped and turned and he pushed me out of the way of the car. A black car. That's all I saw."

"And you?" the officer asked Samantha.

"The same, I'm afraid," Samantha said. "I'm sorry. We were all tired, and nobody was focusing on the car."

The officer shook her head. "Evidently. Well, give us a call if you think of something later."

The male officer rejoined them, and his partner stood up, ready to leave.

"You two might as well go home," he said to Mariana and Samantha. "Your friend is in surgery, massive head trauma and internal bleeding, and it's going to be a long night."

"Ramon was wrong," Mariana said once the officers had gone. "I'm not going to be able to talk with Art before he dies."

"You don't know he's going to die," Samantha countered.

"No. But I just don't think he wanted to live."

"Wants. Wants to live. He's still alive," Samantha said.

Mariana nodded. "Now. You're right. He's alive now. Would you mind just dropping me off at home? I don't live far, and I don't want to go back to the store to pick up my car. I'll find a way to get it tomorrow."

"I'll drive you home now, and I'll pick you up tomorrow,"

Samantha said. She put her arm around Mariana to help her out of the building.

"Mariana!"

They were almost to Samantha's car when Mariana heard someone call her name. She turned in panic, afraid it was somehow Art again, but instead she saw Claybourne trotting across the parking lot toward her.

"I was hoping I'd catch you here," he said when he reached her side. He was a little short of breath.

"Art's still alive," Mariana said. "Why did they call you?"

"Because at the least, it's attempted murder, and it has to be related to the Marconi homicide," Claybourne said. "I don't believe it could be a coincidence. I know you must be tired, but I was hoping we could talk."

Mariana hesitated. "I'm spaced out. And I don't have anything to add to what I've already said."

"Mariana, you must know something. Even if you're not aware that you know it." His eyes held hers. "One glass of wine. That should put you out for the night."

"Alcohol is not a good idea," Samantha said.

"I'll be all right, Samantha," Mariana said. "One glass of wine. And thank you."

"I'll call you in the morning," Samantha said, getting into her car.

Claybourne took Mariana's arm and led her back the way he had come.

The thought that people had been touching her all day came and went. She wanted to lean, and Claybourne's arm felt right to her.

When they reached his car, he opened the door and helped her in.

He waited until he was in the driver's seat before asking,

"Are you really sure you can handle a glass of wine? How do you feel?"

"I feel like an invalid," she said. "Invalid. Not valid. My power has been sapped. And you're right. I have to reconsider the invitation. I won't be able to handle a glass of wine tonight."

"Then let me drive you home."

Mariana nodded. She gave him directions, a few short blocks that she would have walked under other circumstances.

He stopped in front of the door to the building, ignoring the No Parking sign, and turned off the engine.

"I'm not asking you up," she said.

"I know."

She leaned across the space between them to place her cheek against his.

"Mariana," he whispered, his moustache brushing her ear so softly she barely felt it.

"Goodnight. David." She forced herself to say his name.

"Goodnight."

She disengaged without meeting his eyes and got out of the car.

She was inside the building and halfway up the stairs before she heard the engine start and his car pull away.

The sun streamed through the leaded glass window, warming her naked body. The man stood a few feet away, dressed in a dark cloak, his face temporarily hidden as he peered closely at his work.

He was talking, she knew that, but she couldn't hear the words. He wanted her, he needed her, that was the sense of it.

And then another woman was in the doorway, mouth agape as if she were screaming.

The painting fell to the floor. The man turned to the woman in the doorway, his face still obscured.

Then he turned back to her, and she knew him again for the first time.

Chapter Fourteen

The morning was overcast, and Mariana had trouble waking up. Miles was sniffing her face, cold nose nudging her cheek, and Ella was howling in the kitchen. She knew she didn't want to move, knew she wanted to stay huddled in the corner of the bed. It took her a moment to remember why. She had to call the hospital, find out how Art was. And she had to confront the fact that someone had tried to hurt her.

Less than two years earlier, she had lost her husband in what appeared at first to be an accident, but turned out to be an unlikely murder. For the next few months it had seemed as though everyone around her was under attack, especially the members of the channeling circle that included Deirdre, Jerry, and Ramon. And Suzanne, the first psychic to become Mariana's friend, had died in Mariana's arms, a victim of the same damaged soul who killed Tim. Mariana had not been a direct target, though. This time she was. But Art was the one who suffered for it.

A sob froze as a lump in her throat before she could let it out.

Miles nudged her cheek again. She opened her eyes to find his two soft green ones peering closely.

And Ella howled.

Before anything, she had to feed the cats. No matter what was going on in her life, the cats needed to be cared for.

She dragged herself out of bed, fumbled into her blue terrycloth bathrobe, and made it to the kitchen without having to think about anything except Ella howling on the counter next to an empty dish and Miles bumping her calf, threatening to trip her if she didn't go straight to the cat food cans. Only after food was in both dishes, and both cats were eating, did she think about making the phone call to the hospital.

She knew that Samantha had stuck a card with the hospital phone number in her bag. She went back to the bedroom to find it, and Ella started howling again.

"Please," Mariana whispered. "Please, Ella. Not now."

The howling Siamese ignored her. Mariana went back to the kitchen to put her hands on the cat's flanks.

She felt as if it took longer than usual, but the Reiki energy came through her body into her hands, and the cat began to eat again, and to purr.

Even on this cool morning, the sun was coming into the kitchen, warming the apartment.

Despite herself, Mariana felt better. She stayed with Ella until the cat had eaten enough that she paused to wash her face. She gave only a faint protest when Mariana removed her hands.

The slight surge of well-being lasted only until she reached the hospital operator.

"Art Freeman is in the Intensive Care Unit," the woman said. "The only thing I can tell you is that his condition is critical. Are you a family member?"

"No. No, I'm not. I'm a friend."

"Then I'm afraid you can't visit him." There was a practiced note of apology in her voice. "But feel free to call later. Call tomorrow. There probably won't be any change before then."

Mariana thanked her and hung up.

She retreated to her pink meditation chair. She would either have to wait for whoever it was to try to hurt her again, hoping the person would continue to be unsuccessful and wouldn't harm any friends of hers the next time, or go out and look for answers. Guidance would be a help, one way or another.

Ella hopped onto her lap and settled in.

But Mariana's guides were silent. She couldn't even feel the presence of the hawk on her shoulder. The problem was her own, she knew that. The hawk was there, had to be there, she was just too stressed to sense him.

Her mind kept working, she couldn't shunt the thoughts aside, and that was why she couldn't find guidance, she knew that, too. Or else there was something she had to discover for herself. But what? Where?

An image tried to tease its way into her consciousness. Something blue, a blue dress.

Before Mariana could bring it into focus, the phone rang, and the image was gone.

"How are you?" Samantha asked.

"Okay. Thanks." Mariana struggled with a sense of disappointment. She had wanted the caller to be Claybourne. And that was another thing she hadn't thought about, the moment with Claybourne as he had dropped her off the night before. "I called the hospital, and they wouldn't tell me anything about Art. Do you have any connections there?"

"Nobody I could get hold of this morning. I tried. What say I pick you up in about an hour? We can have a real Sunday brunch, and then I'll drop you off to get your car."

"You want to make sure I eat." Mariana didn't have to make it a question. "Okay. An hour is fine."

She hung up the phone. Ella had left her lap when she

172

started talking. Since she still couldn't sense the hawk, she had no excuse to sit. So she got up to dress and prepare herself to meet Samantha. And the rest of the day that loomed, somehow, ahead of her.

Samantha, of course, was on time. Mariana had been watching for her and managed to be waiting at the bottom of the stairs when the car paused, engine idling.

"I thought maybe Mexican food would interest you," Samantha said.

"Grounding, I know," Mariana said. "Beans and rice and fat. I'll try. But what will you eat? Mexican restaurants usually don't have a lot of green stuff."

"I can handle a tostada, just this once."

The restaurant Samantha drove to was a popular place in downtown Ventura. Mariana looked at the crowd in despair. She wasn't particularly hungry, and waiting for a table wasn't going to improve her disposition or her appetite.

Someone was waving at them from a corner of the room.

"Over here. You can join us," Stella called. She and Bernard were sitting at a table for four. He was staring intently at a menu, ignoring his wife's enthusiastic invitation.

"It's up to you," Samantha said.

"Yes. If you don't mind, let's join them. I need to talk to Stella." Mariana sent a mental note of gratitude to the hawk, knowing guidance had appeared, even though she couldn't pick it up directly.

Mariana worked her way across the dining room, excusing herself as she passed perky waitresses dressed in brightly-colored cotton blouses and skirts, somehow more Southern California than Mexican, who were overburdened with their trays of heavy plates. Mariana made a note to be careful what she ordered. Any one of those brunch dishes, swimming in sour cream, cheese, and guacamole, would feed three people with normal appetites.

The smells didn't help. There was an underlying scent of fried animal flesh that curdled her stomach.

She slid into the booth next to Bernard, leaving the spot next to Stella for Samantha.

"We had such a good time yesterday," Stella said. "I hope Deirdre decides to hold psychic fairs regularly."

"This is not the time to decide that," Samantha said. "There was an accident at the end of the day. Art Freeman—I think you met him at the last channeling—was knocked down by a hit-and-run driver in the parking lot."

"How terrible, especially for you, Mariana," Stella said, her tone conveying more curiosity than sympathy. "He was your friend, wasn't he?"

"Mariana knew him longer than the rest of us, but we are all concerned about his condition," Samantha said. "So far, it's critical."

Mariana let Samantha carry the conversation, grateful that she had been spared the task of bringing Stella up to date. She waited until that subject was exhausted and their food was in front of them—she had decided on a tostada, just as Samantha had, choosing greens over grounding—before bringing up her own topic of conversation, the reason she had needed to talk with Stella.

"You mentioned a commune yesterday," she said.

Bernard stiffened. He stared at his coffee cup through his thick glasses. Mariana almost wished she had been sitting across from him, to see his eyes.

"We don't talk much about it anymore," Stella said, frowning at her. "It was a waste of a lot of years of our lives."

"In what way?" Mariana asked.

"We gave control of our lives to the guru," Stella said. "And a lot of money as well. We thought we were part of something bigger than ourselves, on our way to enlightenment, and instead we ended up old and broke and still tied to this existence. That guru is a reptile, I just know it."

"A woman?" Mariana asked.

"No, a man," Stella replied. "A man who started out believing he had a direct pipeline to God, then figured since he and God were one, he could do anything he wanted, all of it the will of God. We swore obedience, and he took advantage. Everything for him, including sex. He went from one close relationship with a newcomer to another. They all do it, of course, but it's still hard to take when you think you were the special one and then discover that your own personal guru doesn't just have feet of clay, he's mud all the way to his neck."

Mariana began to understand why Bernard was so silent.

"That's one of the reasons Eastern religious practices don't always translate well in the West," Mariana said, hoping to take the conversation in a direction less painful for Stella. She didn't want to deal with Stella's pain just then. "In some religious groups, it was okay for monks to have intercourse with very young women as a way of renewing themselves. The monks, not the women. Although they argued that the women benefited from the exposure to the highly evolved monks."

"Pun intended?" Samantha asked.

"Not really. Or maybe. I'm not sure. In either case, it's a view of women that doesn't go over well in America," Mariana said.

"In some circles it doesn't," Samantha said. "The patriarchy is alive and well in parts of this country. You have to admit that Christian ministers have been known to make a very similar argument for sleeping with the flock. Although they usually admit they have sinned, when confronted with the evidence."

"You're talking philosophy, but people were hurt. Nobody benefited but the guru," Stella said, not to be deterred. "Babananda, he called himself. Father Bliss. But he was the only one who got bliss out of the sex, that's for sure. And when you slept with him, you had to be faithful, even though he wasn't. He almost broke up my marriage to Bernard. We lived apart for nearly five years."

Mariana was embarrassed for Bernard, who continued to stare at his plate. She tried to imagine Stella young and attractive and vulnerable to the attentions of a guru. Traces of the person Stella might have been were there, but bitter lines around her mouth were hard to erase, even in Mariana's mind.

"I'm sorry," she said. "You're right, of course. People do get hurt."

"I thought he might come after us when we left, attack us psychically, but Baba-ji says he hasn't done that," Stella said. "Baba-ji says we're safe as long as we visualize ourselves surrounded by white light and golden shields."

"I think you can trust Baba-ji," Samantha said. "No guru, even a false one, is likely to want the karma of psychically attacking former followers, especially when their only sin against him is taking their own power back."

"I hope that's true." Stella shook her head, denying the words as she said them.

"Does the commune still exist? Is Father Bliss still there?" Mariana asked.

"Oh, yes. I heard there weren't as many followers as there used to be, though," Stella said. "He hasn't been able to replace them as fast as they've left. Sort of like smoking. Once you realize you're poisoning yourself, you have to stop. And the word spreads."

Mariana took a moment to think about that. The poison

of the false guru.

"If I wanted to see the commune, is there a way I could do that?" she asked.

"Well, this is Sunday. You could drive out there and ask for the tour," Stella answered.

"The tour?"

"Yes. People who are interested in moving to the commune are allowed to tour the grounds on Sunday, or at least that used to happen. I could give you directions." Stella didn't look happy at the thought. "And you're pretty. You might even get to see Babananda himself."

"Thank you," Mariana said.

She wrote down the directions on the back of a napkin.

Giving directions to the commune did something Mariana hadn't dreamed possible—it silenced Stella, left her with nothing to say. The four of them finished their food with only the conversation necessary for politeness.

Samantha held the question until she and Mariana had paid their checks and were back in her car.

"Why do you want to go to the commune?"

"I won't know until I get there," Mariana replied. "But when Stella mentioned it yesterday, I got a chill, the kind of chill that meant the commune had something to do with me. I thought maybe the reason I can't find a trace of my brother is that he's in a commune. The last time I saw him, he was on some kind of spiritual search, after all. And then there was Umberto's talk of living at the Foundation. That could be a commune. All in all, I think I should check it out."

"I'll go with you."

"No, but thank you for offering. I need to do this by myself."

Samantha glared. "What makes you think this won't be dangerous?"

"Only that it feels right to do it. I don't think it would feel right if it were dangerous," Mariana replied.

Samantha drove into the lot in front of Enchantment and parked her car.

"Call me when you get back. I told Deirdre I'd be in the store today in case Alora doesn't show up. So I'll be either here or home. If I don't hear from you by evening, I'm calling your friend Claybourne and sending him after you."

"Please don't do that. I promise I'll call."

Samantha nodded. "Make sure you do."

The two women went separate ways, Samantha to the store and Mariana to her car.

She paused before getting in, remembering the terrible moment of the night before, when Art had been hit by the car aiming at her. She shut her eyes to see if anything new would come, but no vision arose from her subconscious.

"At least I have somewhere to go," she said aloud.

She got in her car and put the napkin with directions to the commune on the passenger seat so that she could refer to it. Into the hills. She was driving into the hills, and that felt right to her.

The whole trip felt right, including her decision to travel alone.

It took only a few minutes to reach the freeway, first the 101 and then the 126 that took her inland. The sun was shining, and the hills were yellowish brown speckled with green from the little bit of rain that had fallen early in the month.

She left the freeway in Santa Paula, a quaint town that deserved more attention than she could give it, and turned north. The road narrowed to two lanes even before she was outside the city limits.

Once again Mariana found herself surprised by how quickly civilization disappeared, by how much wild territory existed in California right next to the cities.

The road took her in a curve to the northwest, around a lush mountainside with few opportunities to turn off. By the time she reached the one she was looking for, she had gone so many miles that she wondered if she had missed the sign.

But there it was. Retreat to Bliss. A hand-painted sign with an arrow pointing up the mountain, words and arrow noticeably faded.

Mariana turned left onto what could only be called a paved trail, with no space to pull over and no room to pass. She hoped no one was coming the other way.

Another couple of miles brought her to a cleared area with an aged Winnebago parked in it.

A young man wearing a blue work shirt and jeans came out of the Winnebago and waved to her. He was clean-shaven and smiling, with the kind of cherubic face that inspired confidence. Curls of light brown hair fell on his forehead, longer ones graced his neck.

Mariana smiled back. She allowed the engine to idle and rolled down her window.

The young man came to the car and looked at her closely, then nodded.

"Thank you for coming," he said. "Babananda is expecting you."

She was walking through the snow, wearing only a loosely draped orange robe, but she couldn't feel the cold, not on her shaved head, not on her bare feet.

She had promised to follow, and she would follow.

Chapter Fifteen

Mariana stared at the young man. A knot of panic began to form in her solar plexus, but dissolved almost at once. His unwavering smile dimpled his cheeks, and his soft blue eyes met her darker ones easily. She could feel no threat coming from him.

"Babananda was expecting me?" Mariana asked. "How?"

"Babananda has given me discretion in welcoming our guests," the young man answered. "I have several possible greetings to choose from. When I looked at your face, I knew you were a seeker of truth, and that Father Bliss would want to see you. He welcomes seekers personally. And he always expects them."

"Then where do I find him?"

"In the main house. About a mile and a half from here." He pointed along the trail. All Mariana could see was a curve into more greenery. "Enjoy your afternoon."

The young man retreated to the Winnebago and waved again.

She waved in response and drove ahead.

Just beyond the curve, the road dipped into a shallow valley. An area to her right about the size of an ordinary backyard was cultivated with the same late crops she had seen closer to Ventura, plus tall cornstalks and grapevines. No one appeared to be working.

A small cluster of buildings turned out to be nothing more

than a group of trailers plus one battered ranch-style house, hardly what she would have thought of as a main building. She had expected something grander.

She parked her car next to an old pickup.

The front door of the house opened, and a woman wearing the same style work shirt and jeans as the man at the Winnebago came out on the porch. She had the same light brown curls, the same round face and blue eyes, but without the cherubic overlay. Her lips were tight, unsmiling.

"Who are you and what do you want?"

"I want to see Father Bliss," Mariana said. "The man at the Winnebago told me to come ahead."

"I know. Josh called me. But he should have asked who you are first, and what you're doing here." The woman stood at the edge of the porch steps, legs slightly apart, arms across her chest, barring Mariana's approach.

"I was told that the commune is open to visitors on Sunday," Mariana answered. She knew she was evading the questions, but now that she was actually at Father Bliss's door, she wasn't quite as certain why she had come, or how she could explain herself to this hostile guardian of the gate.

"Used to be open on Sunday, when it was a commune. Now it's just the three of us, and we don't get many visitors. Josh stays out front in the Winnebago on Sunday afternoon, though, just in case someone comes. Usually he sends them away." The woman shifted her stance, planting herself and her heavy work boots even more firmly in Mariana's path.

"Just the three of you are here? You, Josh, and Father Bliss?" Mariana asked.

"That's it. After his stroke, everybody else left. Somebody had to take care of him. I chose to stay." The woman's mouth became tighter; her lips almost disappeared.

"I'm sorry. I didn't know he'd had a stroke," Mariana

said. "Would you rather I left?"

"First, tell me who you are and why you came."

"I don't have an easy answer," Mariana replied. "The simplest one I can give you is that I was reading at a psychic fair yesterday, and a woman mentioned that she used to live here, and I got what I thought was a message telling me to come. So I came."

The woman relaxed visibly.

"Okay. That's good enough. It doesn't sound like something anybody would have made up. Maybe Josh was right, maybe it would do Baba good to have a visitor." The woman held out her hand. "My name is Jessie."

"Mine's Mariana." She held the offered hand for a moment, and realized that even as she was checking Jessie's energy, Jessie was checking hers. "Josh is your brother?"

"Yes. My twin. And Babananda is our father. Our biological father," she added.

"Strange. I thought the message to come might mean that my brother, my twin, was here."

Jessie laughed. "No. No one but us. I don't know what you can gain from your trip here. You're a healer, though, as well as a psychic. If Baba can't help you, maybe you can help him."

Mariana almost jerked her hand away. "I'm not doing any healing work these days. And if you can sense healing energy in my hand, then you're a healer. Why would you need me?"

Jessie allowed Mariana's hand to drop.

"Because I've done all I can," she said. "I've been using my own energy, not cosmic energy, and I'm drained."

"Not refueling," Mariana said. "You aren't giving yourself an opportunity to refuel. And you have too much invested in him, that's why it's hard for you to get yourself out of the way and let the energy flow through."

"That's enough," Jessie said, shaking her head. "You can come in."

Mariana followed Jessie into the house.

The living room was furnished with a heavy, overstuffed gray sofa, two matching chairs, and two equally large un-matching chairs—one dark green, the other a black leather recliner. The coffee table, two end tables, and a bookcase were all some kind of dark wood. The effect was one of absorbing all light.

Mariana blinked to adjust to the dimness.

The old man was in the leather recliner.

His face had surely been round at one time, but jowls, dusted with white stubble, pulled his cheeks down toward his chest. Although his white hair had receded from his forehead, curls fell almost to his shoulders. The blue eyes, too, marked him as the father of Josh and Jessie. He was wearing a faded flannel robe over frayed silk pajamas. The flannel sash was knotted loosely over a bulging abdomen.

Mariana hadn't been certain what the guru would look like. To the extent she had tuned in to his vibration through Stella, she had sensed someone charismatic and exciting. Surely that couldn't be the figure she was looking at. She searched his face to find a trace of his former appeal.

Babananda nodded at Mariana as if he had indeed been expecting her.

"Sit down," he said. The words came slowly, with effort. He paused for breath before he continued. "Tell me how you've been."

"I think you may have mistaken me for someone else," Mariana said. "We haven't met."

"But I recognize you," he said.

A golden Labrador retriever got up from beside the recliner and ambled slowly toward Mariana, sniffing.

"I smell of cat," she said to Jessie.

"Get back, Shakti," Jessie said.

The dog paused, looked at Jessie, and sniffed again.

"Back," Jessie said.

Shakti turned reluctantly back to the recliner. She carefully arranged herself again at Babananda's feet.

"Arthritis?" Mariana asked.

Jessie nodded. "Doing well for fifteen, though. Can I get you something to drink?"

"No, thank you." Mariana moved over to the dark green chair. Babananda followed her with his eyes.

"That's good," he said when she was seated.

"Why do you think you might know me?" Mariana asked.

Babananda shrugged. "Remember you from somewhere. Not a mistake. Eyes. The windows of the soul."

"Mariana is a psychic," Jessie said. She had seated herself on the gray sofa, close enough to participate if she wanted to, but far enough that her presence wasn't intrusive. "She received a message that she was supposed to visit you."

Babananda nodded. His pale blue eyes roamed around the room before returning to scrutinize her face. "A dream, then."

"She hoped to find word of her twin brother," Jessie said, "but she only found mine."

"Twin flames," Babananda said. His voice rose above a whisper for the first time. "The true soul mates produce children of the mind, not of the body."

"Now, Baba, you're going to make me feel sorry for myself if you say things like that," Jessie said. "You make it sound as if children of the body are inferior, and here I am, a child of your body."

The old man slowly turned his gaze to his daughter. "Yes. I remember." His voice faded again. "You're here."

"I am," Jessie said. "And so is Mariana, for the moment. You think you dreamed about her?"

Babananda nodded. "I think so."

Mariana waited, but he didn't seem inclined to elaborate.

"I thought the message to visit had to do with my brother," she said. "But there could be another reason I was sent to you. Have either of you heard of a woman called Zelandra?"

Jessie inhaled sharply.

"Damn you," she said.

Babananda opened his mouth, but no words came out. His eyes began to water, and a tear rolled down one cheek.

"I'm sorry," Mariana said. "I'm so sorry. I didn't mean to upset you, I promise I didn't."

Jessie got up from her chair and moved protectively behind her father, one hand on his shoulder.

"Why are you asking about Zelandra? What do you know about her?" Jessie asked.

"Nothing. I've only heard one person mention her name, and then he was murdered. And since then a friend of mine was hit by a speeding car that was trying to run me down. And all I wanted to do was find my brother." Mariana struggled to keep herself from crying.

"Who was murdered?" Jessie's voice was sharp.

"A man named Umberto Marconi. He had come to me for a reading, and then he was found stabbed in the heart in front of the store, and the detective thought it had something to do with me." Mariana's voice broke, and she began to sob.

Babananda's soft crying became a wail.

Shakti lifted her head. The dog shifted position, stretching her paws across the old man's feet.

"Oh, damn. Baba, it's all right. Really." Jessie grabbed a vial of pills from the coffee table, shook a couple into one hand, and picked up a glass of water with the other. "Baba, I'm going to give you something that will make you feel better. I'm going to put two pills in your mouth, and then some water to help you swallow them. Would you do that for me?"

He nodded and the wail stopped as he took first the pills and then the water into his mouth.

"Let me just get him calmed down," Jessie said, "and then you and I can talk outside. I'm giving him a mild tranquilizer. Do you want one?"

"I'd say yes, but I don't know what effect it would have on me, and I have to be able to drive. I don't take much of anything any more. I even have trouble with wine," Mariana said. She shut her eyes to concentrate on slowing her breath.

"Your body is purifying," Jessie said. "It's healthy, but not a lot of fun."

"You're right."

The tranquilizer may have been mild, but it worked quickly. Jessie kept one hand on Babananda's shoulder until his eyes closed and it seemed unlikely that he would start wailing again.

"Okay," she said. "Let's go outside."

Jessie strode purposefully out of the living room without waiting to see if Mariana was following.

By the time Mariana reached the porch, Jessie was several yards away.

"Come on," she called. "It will help if I show you."

Mariana blinked at the brightness of the afternoon and slipped on her dark glasses. The house had been so dim that the sunlight was a surprise. She had hoped they would talk on the porch, but Jessie seemed determined.

The trail Jessie took led up a hillside. Greenery had encroached on the cleared path, so Mariana walked behind, her sandaled feet no match for Jessie's booted ones in any case.

Jessie slowed down when she reached a grassy clearing dominated by a huge ficus. There was a bench under the ficus, but Jessie ignored it. She walked past the tree to the edge of a steep drop-off and waited for Mariana to join her there. The path continued down the hillside, but it was so overgrown that it appeared almost impassable.

The view made Mariana gasp. Purple mountains encircled the kind of valley that must have inspired Shangri-La, verdant growth shining in the afternoon sun. A mansion large enough to be a monastery, with adobe colored stucco walls and a red tiled roof, sat in the middle of tilled fields. A long paved driveway wound from a break in the hills on the far side up to the door of the building.

There was some activity, a silver car arriving and two people being welcomed, but they were too far away for Mariana to make out details.

"She's there," Jessie said. "Zelandra is there."

"Is that the Foundation?" Mariana asked.

"That's one of the names for it."

"Tell me what you know about her," Mariana said. "Please."

"She broke Baba's heart. I know there are some who would say he deserved it, cash karma for the hearts he broke, but he was only careless, he never treated people ruthlessly." Jessie paused to wipe her eyes on her sleeve.

"Do you think she's capable of murder?" Mariana asked.

"I think she's a vampire," Jessie answered, "and the people around her could be capable of anything they believe she wants."

"You don't mean literally a vampire, do you?" When Jessie gave her a skeptical look, Mariana added, "I'm sorry. But I deal with the irrational. I had to ask that."

"I mean she's a psychic vampire, an emotional vampire. She drains energy from people. When energy is low, judgment goes, and people do things they wouldn't ordinarily do. Baba lost his way because of her, lost his way, lost the trust of the commune, lost his will to live. Now everything we had belongs to her." Jessie nodded in the direction of the mansion.

"That was yours?" Mariana asked.

"It was going to be ours, ours for the commune. We established a nonprofit corporation and bought the estate with community funds. Then we woke up one morning and discovered that she was in charge, and Baba had somehow been voted out of his own community, the one he founded and nurtured over the years." Jessie had to wipe her eyes on her sleeve again.

"Why didn't he see it coming? Or someone around him?" Mariana asked. "I know how hard it is to see the truth of what you're involved in, the way fish can't see water. But someone must have seen."

"Of course. But Baba wasn't listening to anyone but Zelandra. He had invited the vampire in, and he was caught by her spell," Jessie said. "Then, of course, he couldn't undo the damage."

"Invited the vampire in. You mean he welcomed the work she was doing, and by the time he figured out what was happening, she was in charge, and it didn't matter what he wanted."

"He was in love with her, and he was sucked dry," Jessie said.

"What about Umberto Marconi? Was she sucking him dry as well?"

Jessie shrugged. "I don't know the name. Whoever he was, he wasn't part of our group. He must have met Zelandra some other way."

189

"If I drove over to see her, would I be inviting the vampire in?" Mariana asked. Another car had pulled up to the door of the mansion, and two more people were welcomed inside.

"You would. Don't do it. Whether Zelandra is connected with the murder and the accident or not, you'd be vulnerable. From what you've told me, you're vulnerable enough already."

"What else can you tell me about her?"

"Nothing. Just stay away." Jessie turned from the cliff and started back along the trail to the house.

"Jessie? How would you kill a psychic vampire?"

Jessie stopped. "What do you mean?"

"Well, traditionally vampires were killed with wooden stakes through the heart. So how would you kill a psychic vampire?"

"I don't know. A crystal stake?"

"That's what killed Umberto. A crystal stake."

Jessie hesitated, and shook her head. "You mean someone thought this person Umberto was a vampire?"

"I don't know. I need to sit," Mariana said. "Can we sit before we start back?"

"Yes. Or at least you can. I'm sorry. You do need a healing, don't you?"

"Unfortunately, I'm afraid I do."

"Baba used to hold group meditations under the tree," Jessie said. "The bench still holds power."

Mariana settled onto the frayed wooden bench and closed her eyes. "You're right."

"I'd stay with you, but I need to get back. Can you find your way?"

"I hope so."

Jessie laughed.

Then it was silent, and Mariana knew she was alone.

The energy came up through her feet, green energy, earth energy. She allowed it to fill her body, fill it until her own energy was flowing again.

Then she opened her eyes and took the path back down the hill to the frame house with its peeling paint. The house had seemed worn down earlier. Now she saw it as barely standing.

No wonder Babananda had cried when she mentioned Zelandra.

Jessie was out of the house and on the porch before Mariana could walk up to the front door.

"I won't invite you in again," she said. "Baba needs to rest."

"I'm sorry I upset him. I didn't know."

Jessie nodded.

"I'm feeling much better," Mariana added. "Sitting under the tree was what I needed. And I want to do something for you. Would you let me offer a few minutes of Reiki? Here on the porch? I haven't given Reiki to anyone but the cats for months, but I'd like to give it to you."

"I'd appreciate it," Jessie said.

Jessie sat down on the steps, and Mariana knelt behind, so that her hands could rest on Jessie's head. Mariana closed her eyes, letting the energy flow through. When it felt right, she moved her hands to Jessie's neck, then her shoulders.

"That's all we can do today," she said.

"Thank you," Jessie said. "I feel better. I'm glad you came."

"So am I." Mariana was going to say something about coming again, but the words wouldn't come out. "And thank you."

Jessie was still sitting on the porch step when Mariana drove away.

The shadows had engulfed the road, letting her know that the afternoon was almost over. She paused when she reached the Winnebago and waited for Josh to come out.

"How was your afternoon?" he asked. "Did you find what you were looking for?"

"Not exactly. But I want to thank you for letting me through." She held her hand out, and he clasped it in both of his.

"You're welcome." He squeezed her hand, then let it drop. "Be careful."

"I will."

She waved good-bye and continued her trek back down the mountain, through Santa Paula to the freeway, and then to Ventura.

By the time she reached her apartment, her energy had flagged again, and she needed a nap. She lay down on the bed, hugging Miles, thinking she would close her eyes for just a moment.

A ringing phone startled her, and her body jerked itself erect to answer it.

"Where the hell have you been?" Claybourne said. "Art Freeman is in a coma, and they don't think he's ever coming out."

She was lying on the floor of the temple, struggling with the haze in her head, trying to work her way to consciousness. The fumes of the potion that awakened her gift of prophecy refused to disperse.

Why was she alone? Where were the others?

The answer came to her as a vision, and when it did, it was so terrible that she willed herself to die.

Chapter Sixteen

Mariana struggled with Claybourne's words.

"Art's in a coma?"

"Yes. I left a message on your machine, and I called the store, too. I didn't worry until Samantha called me back to tell me that you'd gone off somewhere. One more time, where the hell have you been?"

"Oh, God, Art's dying because of me. I can't deal with your anger right now," she said, fighting tears for the second time that day. "And if you talked to Samantha, you know where I've been."

"I'm not angry," Claybourne said, his words at odds with the tone of his voice. "I've been worried. I thought you promised that you wouldn't wander off by yourself."

"I thought I promised that I wouldn't wander at night. And anyway, I wasn't wandering, and Samantha knew where I was going, and I wasn't in any danger."

"Don't move. I'm coming over." He hung up the phone.

Mariana stared at the receiver before replacing it on the bedside table. She would have told him not to come, but now she would have to tell him in person that she didn't want any company but cats and guides right then.

And she couldn't sense her guides, not even the hawk.

Claybourne must have called from a cell phone, because he was knocking at her door before she had done more than get herself a glass of water.

"I'm not inviting you in," she said.

"Then we'll talk standing here," he answered, his voice harsh. His hair was mussed and his eyes were bloodshot, and he looked as if he hadn't slept in days. "I want to know about this trip to a commune, and why you didn't at least let Samantha go with you."

"I drove to the commune because it felt right. I wasn't even certain the commune had anything to do with all this stuff that's been going on. I was hoping I could find out something about Brian." When Claybourne looked puzzled, Mariana added, "My brother."

"I remember," Claybourne said. "Why did you think he might be there?"

"All I can say is that it seemed possible. I know he's somewhere around here, and the commune was as good a place as any to look. But it isn't even a commune anymore. I didn't sense danger, and there wasn't any. I did find out who Zelandra is, and where the Foundation is, but I didn't go over to meet her because that might have been dangerous, and I don't want to be yelled at." Mariana barely got the words out before she was crying again.

"Okay. I'm not yelling." He pushed the door opened and grabbed her shoulders, pulling her in to his chest. "I know this is painful, and I'm sorry."

"Don't let the cats out!" she gasped, struggling.

"Then you have to let me in."

He was already in.

She shook his hands off, made sure the cats were still in the bedroom, and shut the apartment door.

"All right. Come into the living room." Mariana turned suddenly, terrified. "Oh, God, I invited you in. How could I have invited you in?"

"What's wrong?"

"I didn't mean to invite you in. I don't want to invite anyone in right now. When you invite vampires in, they destroy you!"

"Mariana, I'm not a vampire," Claybourne said, backing away. "You know I'm not a vampire."

"I do know that. I'm sorry," Mariana said, hugging herself, working to calm down. "I'm not exactly together right now, and I have vampires on the brain. Jessie called Zelandra a vampire and said her father had invited the vampire in."

"Can we sit?" Claybourne asked. "Who's Jessie?"

Mariana gestured toward the sofa. She intended to take a chair, but sat beside him instead.

"What was once a small commune is now only a sick old man and his two adult children in a neglected house," Mariana said. "Jessie is the daughter, she takes care of him."

"And she told you where Zelandra is."

Mariana nodded. "Actually, she showed me. The Foundation is an estate right next to the old commune."

"Did Jessie know anything about Umberto Marconi?"

"No. Not exactly."

"Tell me the rest of the story," Claybourne said.

"Jessie called Zelandra a psychic vampire, and she said her father, Babananda, had invited Zelandra in. Once you invite a vampire in, you're vulnerable. And how would you kill a psychic vampire?"

"With a crystal stake," Claybourne finished.

"Yes. And I'm sorry I freaked when you wanted me to invite you in. But everything finally got to me."

"I understand. I've been surprised that you've held up as well as you have, as long as you have. This psychic vampire thing doesn't quite make sense, though. If Zelandra is the vampire, why would someone stab Umberto?"

Mariana began to giggle, a childish, silly giggle that she barely managed to control, fearing it would turn to hysteria.

"Doesn't quite make sense?" She gasped the words. "How does this make sense at all? Who believes in psychic vampires?"

Then Claybourne started to laugh. "I thought you might."

"I don't know what I believe anymore," Mariana answered, and then it wasn't funny to her, and she stopped laughing. "If you think of a vampire as a metaphor, of course, then we all believe in vampires, because we've all been around people who drain us, people who exhaust us. Call that a psychic vampire, and I guess I believe in psychic vampires. Anyway, I believe in them enough that I'm glad I didn't drive over to confront Zelandra. I'm tired enough as it is."

"I'll drive out there tomorrow," Claybourne said. "I'm not so worried about psychic vampires that I'll stop investigating the murder."

"Don't go alone," Mariana said. "And don't accept anything to eat or drink."

"I'll take Torres with me. Does not eating or drinking come from the same source of wisdom as not inviting the vampire in?"

"Sort of. But only if you believe in the unified field theory of metaphysics," Mariana said. "Deirdre says I need to connect everything, and I know it doesn't always make sense to other people. Anyway, whenever you take a trip to the underworld, you have to be careful not to eat or drink if you want to come back. The Foundation feels like hell to me, that's why I said that. Tell Torres, too."

"I will," Claybourne said, placating her. "It would be an official call, though, and I don't think she'll offer hospitality. Did you find out anything more today, anything else I should know?"

"I don't think so. But I think it may be time for me to take a look at that crystal, the stake pounded into Umberto's heart." Mariana's stomach lurched at the thought of touching it. And she knew she had to do it. "Now that I have a sense of what the message might be, I'd like to see if I can pick up anything from it. How do we do that?"

"We drive over to the police station, and you come in and look at it. I can't take it out of the evidence bag. I hope the plastic doesn't affect the vibrations," Claybourne said.

Mariana chose to take the remark seriously.

"No, but I'm not certain I can go into the station. Can you bring it out?"

"Why can't you go into the station?"

"Too many vibrations. I'd have to shield myself, and then I couldn't pick up the ones I want to pick up."

"Okay. Come on." Claybourne stood and held out his hand.

Mariana allowed him to help her up. His hand was warm and solid and reassuring.

"Let me get a jacket," she said.

He followed her to the door of the bedroom.

Miles was sitting on the bed. He glared at the intruder, ready to retreat if Claybourne came toward him. Ella had been asleep on the chair. She opened her eyes, glanced at Claybourne, and closed them again.

"Your cats don't seem to want to have anything to do with me," he said. "Most cats like me."

"They're just not used to company anymore."

"That fat brown and white one looks as if I might win him over."

"That fat brown and white one is Miles, and you could probably win him over if you had a piece of chicken in your hand. Ella is a lot tougher, though." Mariana had grabbed a black and gray fleece jacket from her closet. She met Claybourne back at the door.

"Miles and Ella?"

"Miles is laid-back and cool, and Ella has a voice that is not to be believed, especially when she's hungry."

Claybourne laughed. "There was a musician in the family."

"Yes. Shall we go?"

She ushered him out, locked the door, and followed him down the stairs.

The marine layer had chilled the evening air, creating fog halos around the streetlights, and Mariana pulled the jacket closed across her chest.

Claybourne's car was parked so that it blocked the alley.

"Don't the rules apply to you?" she asked.

"Some do, some don't," he answered, opening the passenger door for her. "I was in a hurry."

The police station wasn't far from where Mariana lived. Within minutes, Claybourne was parking in the lot.

"I'll be right back," he said.

He returned shortly with a plastic bag in his hand.

"Do you need some kind of special circumstances?" He handed her the bag. "Or can you do your stuff here in the car?"

"I'll do my best here," she said, "whatever that is. Could we have a little light?"

Claybourne flipped on the overhead bulb and shrugged.

"The best we can do unless you want to go inside," he said.

Mariana examined the bag in the dim light. There were still traces of blood on the crystal, and she allowed the surge of fear from the memory of the bloody corpse to rise in her and then dissipate. The crystal itself was about eight inches long, cracked at the blunt end where someone had pounded it hard enough to penetrate Umberto's body with the pointed end. Five sides showed the rough lines common to natural crystals, but the sixth was unnaturally smooth for most of its length.

"This crystal is incomplete," she said.

"What do you mean?"

"That was the wrong word. But look—you can see where it was either broken or cut, most likely cut. There's another piece of it somewhere, that's what I meant, probably with another point."

Claybourne groaned. "I hope we don't find the other point in another body."

"So do I."

"Anything else?"

Mariana shut her eyes.

"I'm not getting the sense that anyone thought Umberto was a vampire, but I am getting images of figures in black cloaks." She opened her eyes and looked at him. "I may be getting in my own way."

"What do you mean?"

"All the vampire talk, of course." She handed the bag back to him. "I see what you mean about working with psychics not being useful."

"But always interesting. Let me return this, and then let's continue over dinner."

"I don't think—" she began, about to tell him that she didn't think it was a good idea to have dinner, but he was already out the door and heading to the building.

She tried again when he came back.

"I don't think having dinner is a good idea."

"If you mean because of my wife, she moved out yesterday."

"Then I really don't think having dinner is a good idea," Mariana said.

"But will you do it anyway? You have to eat."

"People keep telling me that. I do eat. Really. The question is whether it's a good idea to eat with you." Mariana focused on his hazel eyes, his slightly bloodshot hazel eyes. "I'm too close to the situation to really pick up on what's going on. But it wouldn't take a psychic to see that you've been under some kind of stress."

"And you're leading up to a question about whether my wife and I had been arguing for a long time, and whether the break up had anything to do with this case, right?" Claybourne's mustache twitched, covering a brief smile.

"I told you you were psychic," Mariana said.

"No, but I know something about people. Yes, we'd been arguing for a while. No, she didn't leave because I'm attracted to you, or because I was attracted to anyone else. She left because I was out late too many nights, and she got tired of being alone, and she met someone else. Now, will you have dinner with me?" Claybourne asked.

"Okay. I'll have dinner with you. I'm still tired, though. It has to be a short one. Nothing fancy."

Claybourne nodded. "How about that vegetarian hole-in-the-wall on Main?"

"An inspired suggestion. Not only is the food good, but it's only a couple of blocks from where I live. Thanks."

Mariana shut her eyes for the short trip to the restaurant. Despite having assured Claybourne that she would eat with him or without him, she would probably have fed the cats and gone straight to bed if forced to fend for herself.

But she could handle a bowl of soup and a small salad. And a glass of wine.

The restaurant consisted of one small room with half a

dozen booths and a scattering of tables. Only one booth was occupied.

"Your choice," the woman who greeted them said, gesturing at the open seats. She was solidly middle-aged, with long, graying hair, and she had the comfortable, healthy look of someone who ate her own food. Mariana had seen her there often enough to be fairly certain she owned the restaurant, although they had never talked.

Claybourne led the way to a corner booth, and the woman gave them menus.

Mariana glanced at hers and set it aside.

"Any recommendations?" Claybourne asked her.

"Everything's good. I had already decided on soup and salad, though. And wine. If you're new at this, used to eating something heavy for dinner, you might like the vegetarian chili."

"Or the vegetarian Mexican plate," the woman added.

"That, too," Mariana said.

Claybourne agreed on the Mexican plate.

The woman returned almost immediately with their wine.

"A salad comes with the Mexican plate," she said. "Do you want your salad with his and then your soup with his dinner?"

"That's fine," Mariana said. Once the woman was out of earshot, she added, "I'm sorry about your marriage."

"I am too. But I guess not sorry enough that I chose to do something about it. I saw the breakup coming. And I pretty much ignored the signs," Claybourne said.

"Do you really think the marriage is over?"

"Yes. And I don't particularly want to talk about it tonight."

"You're still wearing your wedding ring, though."

Claybourne looked down at his hand. "I know. I've gained

some weight since I put it on, and I may have to have it cut off."

"I wore mine until I lost so much weight that it was falling off my finger. I took it off because I didn't want to lose it," Mariana said.

"Your marriage ended in a different way. And you lost weight in grief, I gained it. Not grief about the marriage, that's not what I meant."

"I remember—you mentioned that your father had died recently." Mariana felt a flash of energy roll through her, and paused to check the source with the hawk. The hawk was there, and Mariana sent back a flash of gratitude. "Have you talked to him? He's still around, you know."

"Still around? What do you mean?"

"When I mentioned your father, I felt a rush of unconditional love. I don't think of myself as a medium, but I do receive messages sometimes, especially when someone really wants to send love. The hawk says the love is from your father, and you can talk with him in a dream, if you want to." Mariana's face was flushed, both from the energy flow and from the embarrassment of feeling love for Claybourne, not an emotion she was comfortable with right then.

Claybourne shook his head and laughed. "My father sent unconditional love for me and I can talk to him? I'll have to think about that. In a dream?"

"Yes. That's the easiest way. Ask for a dream about your father, and he'll be there."

"Maybe." He took a sip of wine and changed the subject. "You mentioned that you went to the commune hoping for word of your brother. Why can't you get the information about your brother from a dream?"

"I wish I knew the answer to that," Mariana said. "Under the best of circumstances, nothing works all the time. People

203

who want scientific proof of psychic phenomena are always going to be disappointed, because it isn't a science. Somebody said that was the difference between physics and metaphysics. Physics can be replicated every time. Metaphysics can't."

"You said your brother was a twin, though. I thought twins were supposed to have some special kind of psychic bond."

"We did have a bond, especially when we were little, although I don't know that I would have called it a psychic one," Mariana said. "No one talked about psychics in my family. And even when we went in different directions in college, I thought the bond was there, somewhere. I never really believed we could be separate, the way we are now. Brian became enigmatic, though, distant, and I had lost touch with him psychically long before he actually disappeared. It was painful then, and it's painful now."

"No one talked about psychics? Then how did you become one?"

"The ability was always there. I'm not sure one becomes a psychic."

"Okay. Then when did you recognize your ability?"

"I could say last year, although of course I had some childhood experiences that paved the way." Mariana hesitated, but the flow of love had left an afterglow, and she wanted to tell him more about herself. "A lot of psychics will tell you about being a child and seeing a woman standing in the corner of the room, for example, one nobody else sees."

"And you saw her?"

"I did. And so did Brian, even though he didn't admit it. I almost didn't forgive him for not speaking up at the time, when our mother was so mad at me. That was the first rift, I suppose. Brian didn't want her to be mad at him, so he didn't tell the truth, that he saw the woman, too. He finally told me he had seen her when he told me that he was quitting his job and looking for a teacher. I still feel some kind of dislocation when I think about that night."

"What kind of a teacher?"

"A spiritual teacher, a guru." Mariana laughed. "What other kind is there? That's the other reason I thought I might find him at a commune. When he didn't find what he was looking for in Los Angeles, he went on the road, to Hawaii, to Sedona, to Jackson Hole, Wyoming. I thought he might have found his way back here."

"All roads lead to Southern California."

"Something like that. And then Baba-ji said Brian was near, and you know the rest."

"Could your search for Brian have something to do with someone wanting to hurt you?" Claybourne asked.

"I suppose. Although the only people who knew about that before Umberto was killed were the people at the store." Mariana shivered. This time the energy flow wasn't a pleasant feeling. "I don't want to believe that this has to do with anyone at the store."

"All this leads back to the store, you know that, including the attack that missed you and put Art Freeman in a coma."

"I feel so guilty," Mariana whispered.

Claybourne reached across the table, taking her hand.

"Guilt doesn't help," he said.

"I know." She removed her hand from his. "I want to make something clear right now. I became involved with Art Freeman at a time when I was flailing, struggling to find some kind of faith in myself and my abilities. That decision led directly to his injury. I can't change that. But I can approach other relationships, or possible relationships, with extreme caution. For the sake of my own sanity."

"I'll keep that in mind," Claybourne said, but he left his hand near hers. "Maybe we need to find a neutral topic of conversation."

"Or at least one we can argue dispassionately about." Mariana paused to let the restaurant owner deliver their salad plates.

"Enjoy," the woman said.

"Did you enjoy *The Scarlet Letter*?" Mariana asked.

Both Claybourne and the restaurant owner blinked in surprise.

"I had to read it in high school," the woman said. "I loved it."

"I read it in high school, too, and I hated it," Claybourne said. "Why *The Scarlet Letter*?"

"Because everybody who had to read it in high school either loved it or hated it, and everybody remembers it," Mariana said.

"But not well enough to argue over," Claybourne said. "I discovered reading for pleasure when I needed something for a book report and found Robert Heinlein in the school library."

"That'll do it," Mariana said. "Talk science fiction to me."

"*Stranger in a Strange Land*?"

"I loved that one, too," she said.

The restaurant owner walked away laughing.

Heinlein, Asimov, and Clarke got them through dinner, and even the argument over Marion Zimmer Bradley was friendly.

As they were getting ready to leave, Claybourne said, "You only recognize authors from several years back. You don't read science fiction anymore, do you?"

"No. My life is too strange. I can't. I read mysteries because they always have tidy endings."

Claybourne looked at her sadly. "I wish I could tell you I understood your life. But I don't."

She nodded. "I'd like to walk home, if you don't mind."

"I don't mind, but I'm walking with you."

The fog had intensified during their time in the restaurant. The halos around the streetlights had become bright, gauzy clouds.

Five people in black cloaks crossed Main Street in their direction.

"The vampire children," Mariana said.

But when they approached, she realized that she was wrong. Five ordinary people in dark coats had simply been distorted by the fog. The fog had distorted her vision.

She was lying on the table, unable to move, unable to speak. The man with the head of the golden dog stood over her.

She recognized his eyes . . .

Chapter Seventeen

The first call the next morning came from Samantha.

"How are you today?" she asked.

"Better, I guess," Mariana said. "I'm sorry I was too tired to talk last night."

"Why don't you come to my office this afternoon for a Reiki treatment? And some herbal tea to combat stress might be a good idea, too. You can tell me all about your adventure then."

"But the store is closed, and you don't usually work Monday," Mariana said.

"I have the keys to the store, and I'll make an exception for you. Say one-thirty?"

Mariana agreed. She replaced the phone and closed her eyes. Her body felt heavy, and while she had forced it to move enough to get up and feed the cats, she had then gone back to bed. Miles had come with her, ready and willing to spend the day snuggling, but Ella had hopped up on the meditation chair and glared at her.

Ella was still glaring from the meditation chair.

Mariana could feel the cat watching her, and she knew it was time to do something with her day. Even if it was only a meditation with Ella on her lap.

The phone rang again, though, before she had done more than think about moving.

"How are you?" Deirdre asked.

"I'm fine," Mariana answered automatically.

"No, I meant how are you really?"

"Confused. Guilty. Frightened. I don't know," Mariana said.

"That's what I thought. I don't suppose it will do any good for me to tell you that Art's injury isn't your fault."

"No, but I'm glad you believe that," Mariana said.

"Samantha said you visited a commune yesterday, the one where Stella and Bernard used to live. What happened?"

"It isn't really a commune anymore. I met a couple of interesting people and discovered where Zelandra and the Foundation are, but I didn't go over there. Claybourne said he'd check it out today."

"At last he has a lead," Deirdre said. "I hate speaking ill of someone I don't know, but I hope it turns out that this Zelandra is our murderess, and Claybourne arrests her, and the violence ends there. Samantha and I had to clean the store again yesterday. If there is any more blood in the parking lot, I'm going to have to think about selling."

"For more reasons than I can tell you, I hope it doesn't come to that. Did Alora come to work?"

"No, and this time she didn't call. Whatever happens, I don't think I'll be able to keep her. I know you're not sorry about that."

"No, I'm not," Mariana said. "That's the first good news I've heard, in fact."

"Even if I ask you to work behind the counter until I find someone?"

"Even so." Mariana was upright and focused now on the conversation. "Deirdre, I think Alora had something to do with the disasters of the past two weeks. Claybourne and I talked about it last night. He thinks it may have started because someone overheard me saying I wanted to find my brother, the day Umberto was murdered. So someone who was in the store has to be part of whatever is going on."

"You think this has something to do with your brother?"

"I don't want to think that, but Claybourne raised the possibility, and because of the timing, I have to consider it. Even if the threat has nothing to do with Brian, though, it still seems likely that someone from the store is involved. Otherwise, there are too many accidents, and we've been through that before."

"You're right. Everything does point to someone at the store being involved. And you don't want it to be anyone but Alora."

"No. Because the others are Samantha, Jeff, and you."

"And your other clients, Mariana. What about your other clients that day?"

"I don't remember who they were. I'm meeting Samantha at the store for some tea and a Reiki treatment later, and I'll check the card from that day."

"The day before, too. You asked me the day before the channeling if I could pick up anything about your brother."

"Oh, God, Deirdre, this is awful. I don't want to suspect my clients of murder. It's bad enough suspecting Alora, and I don't like Alora."

It was a small joke, but it was the best Mariana could do, and Deirdre laughed courteously.

"Okay," she said. "Let me know if you come up with anything. Or if Claybourne does. I suspect you'll hear from him before I do."

Mariana ignored Deirdre's jibe and again replaced the phone. The idea that someone would want to hurt her was difficult enough to deal with. Adding the possibility that someone at the store was involved, even Alora, made it worse.

Thinking that it might have something to do with her inquiry into Brian's whereabouts was so painful that she wanted to go back to bed and hide until it was time to die.

Instead she got up and took a shower and made a cup of tea. She wished she had some of the stress mixture, but lemon ginger would have to do until she saw Samantha.

To further soothe her nerves, she sat with Ella in the meditation chair. She closed her eyes and concentrated on her breathing, not her thoughts. The telephone interrupted for the third time that morning.

"Well, Torres and I drove up to see Zelandra," Claybourne said.

"And?" Mariana immediately perked up.

"She knew Umberto, said she had heard he was murdered, and she had nothing to add. She didn't seem to know anything about Enchantment or Art Freeman or you."

"You asked her all that?"

"I did."

"What else did she say?"

"Only that if she heard anything that might help, she'd let us know."

"Damn." Mariana rubbed her forehead. Something didn't feel right. "I think she's lying, for what it's worth."

"Maybe. But for now that's a dead end. And there's something else I have to tell you." Claybourne paused long enough that Mariana almost leapt in, then finally continued. "I dreamed about Art Freeman last night. I dreamed he was telling me to protect you from the vampire."

"How did he look?"

"What? In the dream? He looked the way he looked the night of the channeling, except that he was calm."

"Dear Art," Mariana said. "Still trying to protect me. At least he's all right on the level of spirit, whatever is happening with his body. Thank you for telling me. That's the first thing I've heard in days that has made me feel better."

"How do you know he's all right? And how could my dream about a man in a coma make you feel better?"

"Well, he was strong enough in spirit to contact you. He probably knew it wouldn't do any good to try to contact me. And you said he was calm. You're not describing a bloody specter or anything. So he's all right on the level of spirit, and that means his body has a chance," Mariana said. "The spirit does heal first, you know."

"I'm afraid I don't quite share your faith."

"Then ask for a dream about your father and see what happens."

"I'm not ready for that." Claybourne muffled the receiver and spoke to someone else, then came back. "I have to go. One more time, don't wander anywhere. I'll talk to you later."

Mariana hung up without telling him she was going to the store to meet Samantha and check her client list. Time enough to do that if someone from the client list popped out at her.

She sat back in the meditation chair. Her energy had been so high when she left the commune, after the meditation under the tree, but it was gone again by the time she got home. Maybe Samantha could help her understand what was going on.

A few minutes of concentrating on her breath with Ella curled up on her lap calmed Mariana enough that she realized she had to eat something before she met Samantha.

Getting herself together was a good idea generally.

She started by peeling a seedless tangerine, one of the first of the new season, and eating it slowly. A shower that included a chakra cleansing visualization helped. And scrambled tofu on multigrain sourdough toast filled her stomach comfortably.

By the time Mariana was dressed and ready to go, she was looking forward to her Reiki session, if not to the other half of her afternoon task, figuring which of her clients might have been involved in murder and then tried to run her down in an automobile.

Samantha was standing in front of the store when Mariana pulled into the parking lot.

"Promise me you ate something," Samantha said.

"I did. I'm fine, really, or at least as fine as I can be under the circumstances."

"Okay. Then let's get started." Samantha unlocked the door and punched in the code to turn off the burglar alarm.

"I need to do something else first, because I don't want to do it after. I need to look at my appointment cards for the day Umberto was murdered and the day before."

Samantha flipped the light switch, and the overhead lights flickered into brightness. "You think one of your clients was involved?"

"I have to consider it. Claybourne thinks this whole thing may have started because someone overheard me talking about Brian, someone who doesn't want me to find him," Mariana said. "So I have to look at who else was here those two days."

Mariana moved behind the counter and opened the drawer where the current month's appointment cards were filed. She picked up the stack, removed the rubber band, and flipped through until she found the ones she was looking for.

"Names," she said. "I have to associate faces with the names. A couple of them are easy—I remember Kim and Pauline because I needed to keep them apart. But the others, Karen, Jenny, Betty, I'm drawing a blank on those."

"Bring the cards into my office," Samantha said. "Let's do a little relaxation exercise, see if we can't get your conscious mind out of the way."

"You want to hypnotize me?"

"That's what Jeff would call it. I consider meditation de-hypnosis—you're released from the hypnotism of every-day routine. And you're in charge the whole time. Remember the faces if you want, don't if you don't want. Stop the medi-tation whenever you like."

"Then let's try it," Mariana said. "Anything that might help me figure this out is welcome."

The two women threaded their way single file down the narrow aisle between crystals and incense to the back of the store.

Samantha opened her office door and pointed to the chair in front of the desk. "Sit down, take your shoes off, do what-ever else you want to get comfortable."

"No couch?" Mariana asked.

"I told you, this isn't hypnotism. Just sit. And give me the appointment cards."

Mariana did as she was told.

Samantha sat behind her desk.

"Close your eyes and focus on your breath," she said.

Mariana fell easily into the opening of the meditation, which began much the same as the ones Deirdre led to open her channeling. Samantha's quiet voice took her through a body scan, allowing her to release tension in each part of her body.

"Now visualize yourself in a safe place, a secret garden," Samantha said. "Some people are going to visit you there, one at a time, but only if you want them to. The first is Jenny."

Mariana visualized the garden, lush with plants. An image

of an overweight, sixtyish woman in jeans appeared in the greenery.

"I see her," Mariana said. She opened her eyes and looked at Samantha. "I wouldn't normally talk about what happened in a reading."

"I know. This has the same confidentiality as one therapist to another. Now close your eyes and think about Jenny."

"She was a cheerful woman who had fallen in love over the Internet. Nothing unusual there."

"Say good-bye to Jenny. Your next visitor is Karen."

Mariana waved good-bye to Jenny, who immediately disappeared. A waif-like woman with long, dark hair took her place.

"Karen wanted her ex-husband back. Wasn't going to happen," Mariana said.

"Say good-bye to Karen. Your next visitor is Betty."

Karen left, and a heavily made-up woman with dyed red hair appeared.

"Betty wanted her soul mate," Mariana said. "And Betty talked a lot about another psychic who told her she would find him."

"You're frowning," Samantha said in the same quiet voice. "Was there something else about Betty you wanted to remember?"

"Not exactly. It was just the way she talked about the other psychic. I had a sense that she might not be totally honorable, that she might be leading Betty on about the soul mate just to keep her coming back, just for the money. But the thing is, Betty would be the type to go straight back to the other psychic and tell her about me. And Betty came to the psychic fair, too."

"Anything else?"

"Not right now."

"Are you ready to say good-bye to Betty?"

"Yes. And I don't need any other visitors. Except Umberto. I'd like Umberto to visit the garden." As Mariana said the words, Betty disappeared and the small man in the woolen cap took her place. His round eyes stared vacantly, but the wound in his chest was healed.

"What is it about Umberto that you need to remember?"

"That he said he was told to come for a reading. I thought he meant that his guides had told him. He had asked me to name one of his guides, and he said that he was psychic, and so I thought he was talking about a message that had come from a guide, a psychic message. But he wasn't. He meant that someone flesh and blood had told him to come to me for a reading." Mariana let the vision of Umberto fade, and the garden along with it. She opened her eyes and looked at Samantha. "I'm such an idiot."

"I gather there's nothing more you want to do in the garden," Samantha said.

"Well, wait a minute, maybe there is." Mariana shut her eyes and brought the garden back. She then visualized a white-haired woman with a warty face wearing a faded blue housedress. "Umberto's next door neighbor, Hannah Jane, said her daughter was a psychic, but the young couple she lived with both had straight jobs. What if she lives with her son and his wife, not her daughter?"

"This is certainly possible," Samantha said. "What next?"

Mariana released the garden and opened her eyes.

"How about the Reiki session you offered?"

"Fine. Just let me get the massage table set up."

"While you're doing that, I need to do one more thing." Mariana picked up the appointment cards from Samantha's desk. "I need to hear how Betty's voice sounds on the telephone. I don't think she was the person in the background when Alora was calling, but I need to be certain."

"What are you going to say to her?"

"Nothing. If I'm lucky, I'll get a machine. If not, I'll hang up."

Samantha had snapped the table into place and draped a sheet over it.

"Don't do that," she said. "Ask her who the other psychic was."

Mariana shook her head. "I'm not sure I can. All of a sudden I'm afraid."

"And with reason," Samantha said. "But you don't have to be afraid of a voice on the telephone. Make a fearless mudra with your right hand, and hold the phone in your left."

"I know what a mudra is—it's what you do with thumb and fingers while you're meditating, or the clasped hands of prayer. What's a fearless mudra?"

"What the Hindu god Shiva does with one of his right hands, placing it palm out at chest level. The energy comes in the crown chakra, out through the hand, protecting you."

Mariana laughed. "Just what I needed. One more protection visualization. Although I guess it's true, I do need it."

"Make the phone call, then we'll do the Reiki."

Samantha handed Mariana the phone from her desk.

Mariana punched in Betty's number, then held the phone in her left hand so she could make the fearless mudra with her right. She felt the energy flowing into her crown chakra and out through her hand, as promised.

"Hello," the voice said. "No one is available to answer the phone right now. Leave a message at the sound of the tone."

"Damn," Mariana said. "That isn't Betty's voice on the recording. I still don't know."

"Then lie down on the table, accept some Reiki energy, and we'll decide what comes next."

Mariana kicked off her shoes and got up on the table.

Samantha arranged low pillows under Mariana's head and knees, then moved to the head of the table.

"Divine Spirit, I ask to be a vessel of pure energy," Samantha said. "Let thy will, not my will, be done."

Mariana shut her eyes, feeling Samantha's soft hands on her forehead.

"That's nice," she said. "Invoking spirit."

"Hush," Samantha said. "Breathe and accept."

Mariana breathed and accepted for almost an hour before Samantha was finished. By the end, she was not only relaxed, she was confident.

"I need to see Hannah Jane," she said, sitting up slowly, to hold onto her sense of well-being.

"No cup of stress tea?"

"I don't need it now. Can I take some of the mixture with me to have at home if I need it later?"

"Of course. And I'm going with you to see Hannah Jane," Samantha said firmly.

"You don't need to do that," Mariana said, not quite as firmly. She got off the table and slipped her feet into her shoes. "I don't think I'm in any danger from Hannah Jane."

"I don't think so either, but I don't trust you to stop there. And I don't want to have to track down Claybourne to get him to go after you. Although he may do that on his own." Samantha whisked the sheet and pillows from the table, dropped them onto a chair, and dismantled the table with the efficiency of someone who did it several times a week. She pulled a jar of herbs labeled Stress from one of the shelves behind her desk, scooped about half a cup into a small paper bag, and handed it to Mariana.

"Thank you," Mariana said. "I really mean it."

Samantha nodded. "You're welcome. Let's go."

Mariana walked on ahead, through the store and out into the late afternoon sunshine. Samantha caught up with her almost immediately.

"I'll drive," Mariana said.

The trip to Oxnard took only a few minutes, but it was long enough for clouds to begin forming over the ocean. By the time she parked in front of the small triplex, Mariana wished she had brought a jacket.

The crime scene tape was gone, but the apartment still looked deserted. All three apartments seemed grayer, darker than when she had first seen them.

She walked up to the porch where Hannah Jane had first stood and rapped on the door. When no one answered, she stepped back to look up at the window, where she caught a glimpse of the old woman peering out.

"Hannah Jane, I need to talk to you," Mariana called.

"Go away. I'm not supposed to talk to you," Hannah Jane answered.

"You don't have to say much. I just want to know your daughter's name, the daughter who is psychic," Mariana said.

Hannah Jane's face was in shadow, and for a moment Mariana thought the woman would leave without answering. But Hannah Jane leaned forward again.

"Her name is Sally," she said. "But sometimes she calls herself Zelandra."

The room was full of women and children, so many that it seemed they could not possibly all be related, but she knew they were. Her own mother was here somewhere. She would know her by her eyes above the veil.

Before she could reach her mother, another veiled woman grabbed her arm, pulling her off balance, and began dragging her toward the hall.

She had to fight back. She had to find the power to fight back. And suddenly a knife was in her hand.

She watched the veiled woman crumple to the floor, knowing what her punishment would be.

Chapter Eighteen

"We need to call Claybourne," Samantha said once they were back in Mariana's car.

"We need to drive up there and see her ourselves. Zelandra lied to Claybourne. I think she's less likely to lie to me, and if you're willing to go with me, I think we'd be safe." Mariana quietly invoked angels for protection and started the car.

"I shouldn't have taught you the fearless mantra," Samantha said.

"Yes, you should. And you taught me more than that. I got a flash of the garden again, the one I visualized in your office, when Hannah Jane said the name Sally, and there was a person in the garden. Are we still confidential?"

"Of course."

"I read for a Sally, who told me she had a split personality. I did my best to stay shielded when I read for her, so I didn't tune in as well as I usually do, but I think it may be the same woman."

"Just because she visited you in the store and you were safe doesn't mean you can visit her at the Foundation as safely."

"She was frightened that day, more frightened than fear-inspiring. I was uncomfortable because I don't have the skills to deal with a split personality, if she really has one. But I have trouble thinking of that woman as a murderer. Besides,

Jessie didn't think Zelandra was a killer. If someone near Zelandra is out of control, she may be grateful to us for calling it to her attention. She may even help." Mariana negotiated the turn back to Wooley, then the short block to Harbor Boulevard.

"You don't really believe that," Samantha said.

"Do you want me to drop you off at the store?"

"No." Samantha sighed. "Let's go."

They drove past the power plant and the open fields, still green with winter crops. Mariana turned on Victoria to get to the freeway.

"We're going to have to do this a little by ear," she said. "I don't know the turnoff to the Foundation, only the one to the old commune."

"Do you have a map?" Samantha asked.

"In the glove compartment."

"Then we can find it. And I'm calling Claybourne to let him know where we're going." She fished in the purse for her cell phone and Claybourne's business card.

"I hope you have to leave a message," Mariana said.

Claybourne was out of the office.

Samantha left her cell phone number with the desk sergeant.

"Be careful what you wish for," she said to Mariana.

"I don't want him to stop me. I need to find out why Zelandra is trying to keep me away from Brian."

The clouds were settling in around the freeway, limiting visibility. Mariana turned on her headlights and slowed down. The interchange that would take them to Santa Paula came before she expected it, and she had to change lanes too quickly.

"Don't ask too much of the angels," Samantha said.

"I'm sorry. I'll drive carefully."

When they reached the Santa Paula exit, Samantha got out the Ventura County map and folded it so that she could follow their path up the mountain.

Mariana kept her word, driving slowly and carefully up the curving road.

"This is the way to the commune," she said, pointing to the side road she had taken on her last trip. "The road to the Foundation comes from the other side of the mountain, though."

"Okay. Keep going. You watch the road, I'll look for the place to turn. We'll find it."

As it turned out, Samantha didn't need the map. After they had followed the road all the way around the mountain, almost to the place where it would curve down toward Ojai, she saw a sign that had to be what they were looking for. She called it to Mariana's attention.

"What on earth is that supposed to be?" Mariana stopped to look more closely.

"The Sanskrit symbol for *Om* arising from the heart," Samantha said. "But someone added three dots at the bottom that look like tears, or drops of blood. Are you sure you want to do this?"

"No. I'm not sure. But I have to do it anyway."

Mariana turned left, easing the car past the sign, and onto the narrow road. At least it was paved, both wider and in better shape than the one leading to the old commune.

After two miles of twists and turns, the road broke free of the dense greenery. Ahead of them lay the valley that Mariana had seen from the commune hill, and in the center of it was the Foundation building. A handful of lighted windows was the only aid to visibility.

"Here we go," Mariana said.

She felt increasingly vulnerable as the car proceeded into

the open valley, so much so that she reinvoked the presence of the angels and held her right hand in the fearless mudra, driving with her left.

They came to a fork in the road, where one path led to a sweeping circle in front of the building and the other led to a parking lot in back. Mariana chose the parking lot. She could make out the dim shapes of other cars, but she couldn't be certain how many or what kind they were. She hoped none was a black car with a dented fender.

The two women got out of the car and walked around to the front door.

Mariana rang the bell.

When nothing happened, she rang again.

She was considering trying the knob when the door opened.

A young woman dressed in black stood there, backlit from the hall light.

Mariana realized that she knew who it was, even before the woman spoke.

"Mariana! Samantha! What are you doing here?" Alora asked.

"We came to talk to Zelandra," Mariana said.

"She doesn't see anyone without an appointment," Alora said.

"Tell her I still don't think the Devil owns her soul. But I have to speak with her," Mariana said.

Alora hesitated. "I'll see what she says. You'll have to stay on the porch, though."

She shut the door without waiting for an answer.

"Someday I will be able to laugh at her," Mariana said.

"I believe that," Samantha said. "I wish I could believe that Alora will live long enough to outgrow her rudeness."

The door opened again.

"Zelandra says she'll see you, so come on in," Alora said. Her voice made it clear that this wasn't her choice.

Mariana stepped inside, with Samantha following.

The room they entered was so large that it must have taken up a third of the mansion's ground floor. The sense of size was greater because the room was almost bare of furnishings. A low platform at one end with a lectern draped in white cloth, as if it were an altar, drew Mariana's eyes. The wall behind it had large portraits of Jesus, Buddha, Krishna, Moses, Mohammed, and a sixth one of a bearded, robed man whom she couldn't immediately identify. Heavy green floor pillows were stacked along two walls.

Before Mariana could move close enough to identify the sixth portrait, Zelandra entered from the door immediately behind the altar, sweeping to a point just to one side.

The woman's face was barely the one Mariana remembered. Zelandra's makeup was now dramatic, eyes heavily framed with liner and mascara, and the full, frizzy black hair no longer seemed out of place. She was wearing a black silk caftan with a border in red of the symbol that had caught Samantha's attention on the road sign, *Om* arising from the heart, with the strange drops below. A two-inch crystal dangled from the V-neckline. The image was a striking departure from the business-suited one Zelandra had presented when she came to Enchantment. Mariana wondered if the split personality Sally had claimed was in fact real.

"Mariana, good to see you again," she said, adding to Samantha, "I don't believe we've met."

"Samantha has an office at Enchantment," Alora said.

Mariana felt diminished, standing in front of the platform. Zelandra had clearly chosen the setting carefully.

"What can I do for you?" Zelandra asked.

"Where do I start? You told Detective Claybourne that

you didn't know me," Mariana said, a surge of anger propelling her voice. "Why did you do that?"

"I hoped you would believe it. I hoped you would stay away," Zelandra replied.

"Stay away until one of your minions managed to kill me?" Mariana asked.

"You don't understand," Zelandra answered. "I wasn't trying to kill you. I came to see you that day, as Sally, because I wanted to know what the fuss was about, but I wasn't trying to kill you."

"Then who was? What is the fuss about? Is this really about me wanting to find Brian? Is he here?" Mariana stopped talking because Zelandra was staring intently at her, and she was losing her anger.

Zelandra considered her response, then turned to Alora.

"Why don't you take Samantha to the kitchen for a cup of tea? I have some things to discuss privately with Mariana," she said.

"I'd rather stay," Samantha said.

"But I would rather you left, and Mariana has come to me for information," Zelandra said. "Mariana will be fine, you have my word, although she isn't going to be happy with what she's going to hear."

"Your word isn't very good," Mariana said.

Zelandra shrugged her shoulders and waited.

"Could we compromise?" Samantha asked. "I don't want tea. I'll wait just outside the door. On the front porch."

"You won't be comfortable, but you can do that if it makes you happy," Zelandra told her. She waited until Alora had escorted Samantha back to the front porch and added, "I don't want you here either, Alora."

Alora started to argue, but Zelandra held up her hand and pointed to another door. Alora bowed her head and left.

"Congratulations," Mariana said. "You at least have Alora under control."

"I have many things under control," Zelandra said. "Not everything, unfortunately. Now, come sit beside me."

Zelandra sat on the edge of the platform, arranging her long skirt around her legs. She patted the spot next to her.

Mariana moved gingerly to the spot indicated, then sat a few inches further away. Her eyes fell upon the folds of Zelandra's skirt, the Sanskrit word and the bleeding hearts. She wanted to say something scathing about the misuse of sacred symbols, but that wouldn't get her the information she needed. She still didn't feel threatened by Zelandra, and that in itself was making her nervous.

"Okay, what's the story?" she asked. "And where's Brian?"

"There is no Brian Edward Field," Zelandra said. "If I tell you that he's dead, will you leave and never come back?"

Mariana's throat closed and her stomach knotted. She forced the breath through her vocal cords.

"I don't believe you. If he's dead, then why was Umberto murdered?"

"To protect the secret of your brother's death and rebirth," Zelandra said. "The man who was your brother is now known as Ishvara. He answers only to that name."

"Ishvara. That's one of the Hindu names of God, but I don't remember which one."

Zelandra smiled faintly. "Ishvara is the aspect of God known as the Personal God."

"Brian is saying he's the personification of God? I don't believe it!"

"This is not Brian. Look at his picture if you don't believe me." Zelandra gestured at the wall.

Mariana got up and looked at the sixth portrait. Under the

hair and the beard and the robes, somewhere behind the brown eyes, was a trace of the Brian she remembered. A small plaque at the bottom of the frame was inscribed Lord Ishvara.

"What have you done to him?" Mariana whispered.

"Nothing has been done that he didn't want," Zelandra answered. "Brian Field died and was reborn as Ishvara. I have only given him the structure that he needed, this house and the people in it, as the place from which his message will be sent forth."

"How did the two of you come together?"

"It was foreordained," Zelandra said. "We are soul mates, two halves of one whole."

Mariana's body jerked.

"I don't believe you. I don't believe you for one minute. Brian is my twin brother, and he is not your soul mate."

"You see," Zelandra said, nodding, "that's why he didn't think you should come here."

"Brian didn't want me here?"

"No. Ishvara was afraid you would complicate our life— the one life that the two of us share—and thus complicate the spreading of his message."

"Are you trying to tell me that Brian really believes he is some kind of spiritual leader?"

"I am telling you that Lord Ishvara has seen his purpose on earth clearly, and that purpose is to unite troubled souls with their destined, eternal mates and thus raise the consciousness of mankind."

Mariana shook her head. "I need to talk to him."

"I have to warn you, if you insist on seeing him, be careful how you address him. His anger is a terrible thing to behold."

"Oh, God. Please don't tell me that Brian is responsible for Umberto's murder and Art's coma, that Brian was trying to have me killed." Mariana sat back down on the edge of the platform, as far from Zelandra as she could manage.

"I warned you that you wouldn't like what you heard," Zelandra said.

"Start from the beginning," Mariana said. "Go back to when you met him, before he was Ishvara."

"I met him in Hawaii, almost two years ago. He was on his way to India, in search of enlightenment, and I was simply on vacation. At that time I had an office in Ventura and a thriving practice as a professional psychic."

"You were already Zelandra then, up from Sally. Is that why you don't have a Sanskrit name? I would have expected you to profane a name of the Divine Mother." Mariana smiled. "A slip. Sorry. I meant choose a name."

Zelandra glared. "We've discussed the possibility of a name change, even though I have established a clientele as Zelandra. Although a name change isn't necessary to symbolize our bond. Ishvara—then Brian—and I connected immediately, both knowing that something profound was occurring. He went on to India, and I came back here, but we stayed in touch by almost daily e-mails. I experienced with him his transformation to Ishvara."

"He found some fake guru?" Mariana asked.

"Please," Zelandra said, shaking her head. "He found a guru, yes, fake or not, and some heavyweight ganja. Your brother wanted instant enlightenment. After a year of dissatisfaction with his meditative progress, he used other means to open the door to cosmic consciousness."

"He burned his brain. That's what you're telling me, he burned his brain on drugs, and now he has some kind of megalomania."

"Do you want to hear this?" Zelandra asked.

"Yes. I'm sorry. I'll try to keep quiet."

"I wanted to have a base of operations ready when he came

back, and it seemed that taking over an existing group would be the fastest way to go. I did some exploring of the local options and decided that this house was ideal. Babananda was old and vulnerable. He had money, money enough to buy this property, but he was losing his followers, and he hadn't yet moved in. I came just in time." Zelandra smiled as if she were proud of her efforts.

"I know the next part from Jessie," Mariana said.

"You know Jessie's version of it, but that's all right. However it happened, Babananda turned what was left of his organization over to me. I was here in this house, ready, when Ishvara came back six months ago." Zelandra stood and walked over to the portrait. "I painted this. Do you like it?"

"Six months ago. Then Brian and I moved to this area at the same time," Mariana said, avoiding her question. In truth, she hated the portrait. "Like it or not, Brian has a connection with me still. Let's go to two weeks ago. I had a vision of Brian, stabbed through the heart. Then the next day Umberto was stabbed and his body dropped at the door to Enchantment. Why?"

"That was the day after the ceremony. Ishvara and I celebrated our oneness in front of this altar." Zelandra pulled the neckline of her caftan down enough so that Mariana could see the crystal more clearly. It wasn't part of the dress, as Mariana had thought. The crystal hung from a gold loop that pierced the flesh of Zelandra's chest. The area was still red and inflamed. "This is half of a twin flame crystal. Ishvara wears the other half in his own chest."

"So I got an image of a dead Brian because he saw his old life as dead? Is that what you're telling me?"

"I think so. There must have been some kind of psychic energy slipping through." Zelandra frowned. "Although Ishvara thought his link with you had been broken long ago.

You came to our attention because one of my clients went to you for a reading that day, then came here to tell me about it. She also overheard you discussing a vision of your brother."

"Betty, the woman who wanted a soul mate."

"Yes. So I asked Umberto to make an appointment and investigate. While you were reading him, he was reading you."

"Umberto said he wanted to live with you." Mariana suppressed a twinge of sadness, remembering the man. She didn't want to be distracted. "He was in love with you, wasn't he, and he didn't believe that you and Brian were soul mates. In fact, he picked up on my connection with Brian. He made the mistake of confronting you about it, that was the disastrous decision."

"He didn't confront me. He confronted Ishvara. Ishvara reacted in anger. I thought we should quietly bury Umberto —no one would have missed him—but Ishvara disagreed. He ordered the body dropped on your doorstep, hoping you would understand that Umberto's body, killed by the twin flame crystal, meant that you should consider your twin brother dead."

"Umberto was Brian's idea of a surrogate corpse, in some way fulfilling my vision?"

"Yes. When you were too dense to understand, I asked two members of our community to pick you up the following Saturday. They made what appeared to be the mistake of picking up Alora. She, however, has embraced our cause."

Mariana nodded. "It was your voice I heard on the telephone. And you stopped by the psychic fair, too. How did you go from wanting to talk with me to trying to run me over?"

"The speeding car—Alora's car—was not intended to do anything more than frighten you. The man who was hit got in the way. He was evidently picking up some kind of vibrations of danger, but they were distorted by his feelings for you."

"I knew that much. Alora hit him?"

"She wasn't driving the car. One of our members, one of those who had spoken with her the week before, was with her. She has, in fact, found a soul mate of her own."

Mariana bit her lip to avoid saying something sarcastic about Alora's new friend. She was still having trouble accepting that Brian might be a murderer, and dumping her anger on Alora and her supposed soul mate wouldn't help.

"Now may I see Brian?" Mariana asked.

"Ishvara knows you are here. He will reveal himself when he is ready," Zelandra said.

"Are you ready?" The voice was a whisper that somehow filled the room.

Mariana jerked around, looking for the source.

"Hidden speakers," she said. "Don't pull the Wizard of Oz stuff. Please."

Zelandra smiled.

The door behind the altar opened, and a man stepped through, a man with flowing dark hair and a full beard, wearing a black caftan that matched Zelandra's, including the symbols at the bottom, with a matching crystal on his chest.

If she hadn't examined the portrait, Mariana would have had trouble recognizing this person as Brian. She stood up and took a step closer, then changed her mind. She didn't want to be within touching distance. He was taller than she remembered—platform heels immediately sprang to mind—and his eyes were wild and bloodshot.

"Brian, what have you done?" Mariana's voice faltered.

"I am Ishvara," he whispered. "I have embraced my soul mate and with her I have embraced my purpose on this earth, which is to unite every soul with its other half, so that we may together create a new race of gods that will never die."

"You have a fever," Mariana said. In his presence, her old link with him wasn't completely restored, but it was strong enough that she could feel the heat from his body. "I think your pierced chest has become infected. Zelandra's chest hasn't healed properly, and I don't think yours has either."

"I have a vision," he whispered. "A vision of every soul united with its other half."

"If your vision is a true one, bring it down to earth in the right manner. Stealing from one man and murdering another and putting a third in a coma are not the right means to establish a paradise on earth. Or anything else on earth except the continuation of what we've got. How can what you've done make things better?" Mariana felt a rising sense of desperation as she realized that her words weren't penetrating.

"I will find your soul mate, the man you have spent many lives with," Ishvara said, "and you will understand."

"Brian, I've spent lives with you, I've spent lives with Tim —you remember Tim, my husband, he's dead—and I've spent lives with at least two other men that I can figure out from my dreams about them, about their eyes. I don't have a single soul mate, and neither do you," Mariana said. "You and I are as much soul mates as you and Zelandra, or as Tim and I were."

"You fought for Ishvara in past lives," Zelandra said, "but he was meant to be mine. Always."

"I remember your soul mate," Ishvara whispered. "But if he is already dead, then you must go to join him."

"No. This has gone far enough. I'm leaving." Mariana glanced down to make certain that she wouldn't trip at the edge of the platform and began backing away.

Ishvara stepped forward with his arm outstretched, but she evaded it.

"I don't want you to leave," he said. "Zelandra will make

certain that you don't."

"Zelandra promised that nothing would happen to me," Mariana said.

"She's right, Ishvara, I did promise. You may go, Mariana," Zelandra said. "You know your way to the door."

Mariana continued to back away from them, and her right hand shot up into the fearless mudra as she did so. She dropped her hand to open the door, stepped through quickly, and shut it again behind her.

Samantha was standing on the porch, shifting restlessly from one foot to another.

"What happened?" she asked. "I was considering coming back in after you."

"We have to get out of here. Did Claybourne call you back?"

"No. And I haven't been able to reach him. I can't call out. This must be a dead spot for cell phones, because of the mountains."

"Then let's just leave." Mariana started down the drive to the parking lot, but she realized that Alora and her friend with the multiply pierced face were blocking the path. "We'll have to go the other way."

"Where?"

"Up the hill to the old commune. We can call for help from there." Mariana cut across the lawn, away from the parking lot, hoping she could hit the edge of it fairly close to the path she had seen from the top of the hill.

"I'm too old for this," Samantha said, attempting to trot along behind her.

"Don't talk, breathe," Mariana said.

She tried to visualize the valley as it had looked from the commune, visualize where the steep path down the hill had melted into the grass. The sun was below the mountain to the west, and only a faint glow illuminated the area. They wouldn't have that for long.

"You can't leave, Mariana!"

Mariana glanced back to see Brian standing in the doorway. He started walking toward them.

"You can't leave," he shouted again.

"Hurry, Samantha," Mariana said. She spotted what she thought was the path and plunged through a flowerbed toward it, Samantha following.

They struggled for footing in the dim light.

Mariana didn't look back again, but she was certain Brian was coming after them. She didn't know whether he had a weapon. She did know that he was sick enough to be out of control.

There was a shadow above her that she hoped was the meditation tree. She had trouble breathing, and forced herself to concentrate on keeping her lungs moving so that she could control her feet.

An unexpected rock caused her to stumble. Samantha, who was also having trouble with her breath, grabbed her arm and kept her from falling.

Mariana stepped on, pushing overgrown shrubs out of her way, peering at the path, knowing that she didn't dare twist an ankle or Brian would catch up.

"Ahhhhhh!"

The cry, full-throated as a lion's roar, came from above them.

Mariana looked up and saw Babananda at the top of the hill. He was standing in a last ray of sunlight, wearing a white robe. His arms were spread, and some kind of long staff was in his right hand.

"Babananda, don't!"

That was a woman's voice from below.

"I'm the one you're angry with! Don't hurt him!"

Mariana glanced back to see that Zelandra was running after Brian, who was now at the foot of the hill.

"Ahhhhhh!" came the roar from above.

The sound was powerful enough to stop all four of them, rooting them to the spot.

Babananda raised his staff. He held it in the ray of dying sunlight for a moment, then hurled it.

Mariana and Samantha both dropped to their knees, but the staff sailed past them.

Brian screamed and fell to the ground.

"Ishvara!" Zelandra cried, rushing to cover the few steps that separated her from him.

She knelt beside his fallen body, placing her hands on his heart. Then she held up bloody hands and began to wail.

Mariana grabbed Samantha's hand and pulled her upright. Babananda had disappeared, but now she knew where they were going.

Both women were panting when they reached the top of the hill. They walked the trail to the house in silence.

Mariana knocked on the door.

"Mariana!" Jessie said as she opened it. "What are you doing here?"

"We came from below," Mariana said, gasping for breath, "from the Foundation, from Zelandra. But you must have known we were coming—didn't Babananda tell you when he came back?"

"Came back from where?" Jessie asked, puzzled. "What do you mean? Babananda is asleep in his chair."

Epilogue

Hello!

Hello, Dorothy, Mariana thought as she climbed the stairs to the park. *Hello, Hiram. Hello, Walter.* She nodded at each of the bronze plaques as she passed. When she reached Dorothy's grave, she settled cross-legged under the tree beside it.

I'm sorry I haven't been here for a while, Dorothy, but life has been complicated. Mariana sent the thought without expecting a reply.

Hello, Dorothy sent again.

Mariana decided Dorothy meant that as encouragement. She opened her mind to Dorothy, feeding her images of the people involved, starting with Umberto and ending with Brian.

Dorothy sent back an image of a happy family.

It's not that easy, Dorothy, Mariana thought. *A family is a Humpty Dumpty thing. Once it's broken, you can't put it back together.*

Hers had been broken for a long time. She realized just how seriously when she tried to grieve for her brother and discovered that her tears for him had been shed long before.

And then, too, his spirit had visited her in a dream, letting her know that he understood the mistakes he had made, and he was sorry for the pain he had caused. There was something about communicating on the spirit level that lessened the impact of worldly losses. Mariana wasn't quite used to that, but she knew it was true.

The hardest part had been driving down to Orange County to see Linda and Todd, less than a month before Thanksgiving, to tell them what had happened to Brian. Or as much as she could tell them.

According to the autopsy, Brian's body was weak with infection. He had fallen against a rock and driven the crystal into his own heart. The autopsy had it all wrong, of course, but since Babananda's staff left no mark, it was the best the medical examiner could do.

Linda cried. Todd stared at the blank screen of the television set. Neither one had much to say.

Mariana gave them what comfort she had to give—her dreams were of no value to her parents—and came home to her cats and her own unanswered questions.

Jessie and Josh were taking over the Foundation, since Zelandra, who was Sally again, was in jail for her part in Umberto's murder. Jessie wanted Mariana to join them, and the idea of a true spiritual community appealed to her. The question was whether they could keep it true, when so many others, including Babananda, had failed.

Claybourne wanted to explore the possibility of a relationship. The question was whether Mariana wanted to. In past lives, she hadn't always had a choice, she hadn't been his equal. This time she had control.

Then, too, there was the image she had of Claybourne standing over Brian's dead body. There was a past life echo there that she didn't understand and didn't like. Baba-ji had said Claybourne might stumble over the murderer. He hadn't literally done so, but something about her relationship with him had.

Deirdre had a message from Art's spirit saying he wanted

out of the coma, but he needed help and wanted Mariana's healing energy. Mariana had hoped in vain that Samantha's energy and skills would do it. The question there was whether, if she helped Art to heal, she could heal herself. That was the easiest of the three. She had to try.

The November morning was clear. The sun was shining, the sky was bright blue, and the waves glistened. One small sailboat glided toward the horizon.

Good-bye, Dorothy, Mariana thought.

Good-bye.